Enjoy!

Stuart Braddon

Red Quill Publishing

DAYTONA DIRT

by Stuart Bradow

Red Quill Publishing
Enterprise, Florida

DAYTONA DIRT
Published by Red Quill Publishing

All rights reserved.
Copyright © 1998 by Stuart Bradow

Library of Congress Catalog Card Number: 98-92243
ISBN 0-9668159-0-4

PRINTED IN THE UNITED STATES OF AMERICA

Dedicated to my wife and daughter, who soothe my aches after tough races. And to my fellow riders, whose good humor and willingness to absorb self-inflicted punishment in pursuit of happiness is a constant amazement. Thanks to my co-workers and friends who pointed out many ways to improve this story. And a special thanks to Helen Collins, who taught me more about writing fiction in thirty minutes than all of my English literature teachers combined.

This is a work of fiction. All characters are either used fictitiously or invented by the author. Most of the events in this book are imaginary. However, Bike Week and the Alligator Enduro are very real.

CHAPTER I

A soggy spring morning dawned in the remote Florida woods. The day before, a thunderstorm had come, beating the forest with rain and lightning. Not that anyone had noticed, out here in the middle of nowhere. The cool morning air would soon surrender to a scorching sun. By then the fog would burn off. But now it lay over the palmettos like a gauze shroud. Trunks of slash pines punctured the mist, then disappeared in the milky sky. Through the stillness, the sound of a high-revving engine steadily increased. The noise rose and fell in abrupt bursts. It sounded like a chainsaw on steroids, getting closer. A motorcycle flashed between the trees. The race was on.

Being the first rider meant that Mark Jemison had no good trail to follow. He was relying on the black and orange course arrows. They were fastened to trees, fence posts and anything solid enough to hold a staple. Each minute of the race another five riders would launch from the starting line behind him. Their knobby tires would tear away the leaf litter and create a narrow winding trail. Out in front, he was on his own.

Mark Jemison had left on Row 1 of the Sand Pine Enduro at precisely 9:01 a.m., Eastern Standard Time. It had been an uphill fight ever since. The course was so tight he felt like he was in a pinball machine. To make things worse, his vision was blurred by wet goggles and the dozens of spiderwebs he had picked up with his body and helmet. Their sticky remains were mummifying his riding gear. A top "A- Class" rider, Mark was very fast through the woods. But staying on time in these conditions was not possible. He could feel the penalty points building as he went. A twenty-four mile per hour average was required. Not a chance.

The liquid-crystal display on his handlebar-mounted race computer read simply "FASTER". He glanced down at the instrument and muttered, "Tell me something I freakin' *don't* know". Brush ripped at his plastic armored body as he plunged into a brushy section of trail. He opened the throttle hard every chance he got. With one quick move he yanked one of the clear plastic protectors off his goggles. Immediately, a dew-drenched palmetto crashed into his helmet, soaking him for the umpteenth time. The sharp edges of the stems raked his forearm. Blood and profanity leaked out of him. Again.

To miss the trees, Mark pitched his

2

motorcycle back and forth with surgical precision. The front tire was the scalpel, the rear a dirt-spitting counterbalance. When the trees were too close together, he lifted the front wheel, turned the bars to reduce width, then slammed himself forward to accelerate. To the uninitiated, he looked completely out of control. But this was a well practiced, high speed ballet. Man and machine kept ripping along, over and through obstacles without hesitation. The fear factor was pushed to the back of his mind. Fear killed speed, and he needed all he could muster.

Glancing down again at his computer, he was startled to see a large spider squeezing into a vent in his chest protector. The hairy three-inch legs met at a grotesque fat body. Huge black fangs hung from its head. Mark Jemison hated spiders, especially the king-sized ones. He slammed both brakes at once. He missed a turn, centerpunched a tree with his right handguard and nearly crashed. Still fighting for control, he smashed the spider with his left hand. Its body exploded against the chest protector and fell off. A splatter of brown juice ran down the plastic. "Shit...just what I needed" he complained aloud, wiping his glove on the nearest tree. He gritted his teeth, opened the throttle and shot forward.

As he left the planted pines and turned onto a logging road, Mark fanned the clutch to build revs, then released it and pulled a long wheelie. At least his Yamaha was running flawlessly. The brutal acceleration was narcotic. He felt invincible with fifty horsepower between his legs.

At the end of the clear-cut, the course arrows pointed back into the woods. Weighting the right footpeg and extending his left leg for balance, he executed a perfect powerslide and made the turn. The trail went straight for a good hundred yards. He made the most of it, speedshifting through the gears at full throttle. No time for the clutch, he thought. The G-forces made him grip the handlebars tighter to stay forward, over the gas tank. Chopping the throttle for the next bend, he saw what looked like another long strand of spider web across the trail. Too late to avoid it, he braced for the turn.

Suddenly, Mark Jemison felt the world yanked out from under him. He was suspended above the ground, still moving, but no longer on his motorcycle. Between the toes of his riding boots he watched the Yamaha leaving. But the projector in his brain was screwed up, it had switched to slow-motion. He could see each knob on the rear tire rotating, each spoke glinting momentarily in the pale sun. He felt no pain, no sensation of any kind. He thought for a moment that he was dreaming. If so, it was a nightmare. His body wouldn't respond. Terrified, he hit the ground and skidded to a stop.

His eyes were fixed on his gloved right hand. Two dislocated fingers pointed straight up, in a grotesque peace sign. It was the last thing Mark Jemison saw as he lost consciousness. His neck had been snapped. A mortal wound pumped fountains of blood from severed arteries. A red halo fanned out across the sand around him. Then he died.

CHAPTER II

As a public defender, Mitch Clanton was accustomed to dealing with other people's problems. His clientele ranged from the homeless to the hopeless. They were people balancing on wires without nets. Mitch strengthened their flimsy grasp on the hem of society. Eloquent, sharp and self-assured, Mitch worked the system flawlessly. He got his clients out of difficult scrapes and let them keep what little they had, including some dignity. It wasn't easy. But the job suited him. Helping the disadvantaged appealed to his sense of fair play. So he usually picked the worst cases that came in.

Going to law school had been mostly his father's idea. At the time, Mitch had been a lot more interested in chasing girls. It didn't hurt that the college he attended had twice as many female students as male. Despite the distractions, he graduated near the top of his class. But college days were just a blurred memory now. Middle age was coming at him like a low limb on a blind curve.

He was determined to duck it as long as he could.

Twenty years ago, in high school, Mitch and his friends had been bitten by the motorcycle bug. Some of them took summer jobs to earn cash for a bike. Others pestered parents for the necessary tender. Dirt bikes were street legal then. As teenagers, they motored all over Florida, entering every off-road race they could find. As they grew older, some of his friends lost interest in motorcycles. Mitch Clanton never got it out of his system.

Now he had a lopsided, love-hate relationship with dirt biking. Nothing in his life was as physically punishing as competing in enduros. Practicing, wrenching his own bike, traveling and competing consumed a large part of his life. Less time for the other things. Like fishing, surfing, women. And each time he left the starting line, he knew he had to risk injury to do well. But he had an addiction to the mental high of racing. He was a speed junkie. For four hours, each race made him live at full speed, in total concentration. Not the everyday slowed down version of life. Then there was trickle of endorphins. Good old pituitary gland. It vanquished pain and made him feel stupendous. Not entirely unlike sex. A shrink could have a field day with the sport, he figured. It drove him to stay in shape, to fight off the passing years. "Ride Hard or Die" had become his mantra against aging. At six-one and a solid one-eighty, Mitch Clanton exercised religiously. Riding with his friends and beating most of the younger riders on any given Sunday was keenly satisfying. Now closing on 40, the trails seemed tougher. The younger racers were getting harder to catch. He tried to shrug it off, but it was a bitter pill indeed.

He had been elected to the top position of FDRA, the Florida Dirt Riders Association. It was the state's largest off-road motorcycling group. He hadn't really pursued the title. It was bestowed on him for his years of devotion to the sport. His duties were usually routine matters such as rule making and being sure the monthly magazine got published on time. But this Sunday morning was different.

Mitch was at the starting line of the Sand Pine Enduro. Almost twenty minutes had gone by since the radio call. He still didn't know what had happened. The news from the first checkpoint was not good. Two riders on the first row had shown up in a state of near hysteria. The youngest was a fourteen-year-old boy, riding only his second enduro. He was in tears. The other rider, a race-seasoned female in her mid-twenties, had blood all over her gloves and pants. They told the checkpoint workers to call for help. All Mitch knew was that a rider was down and might be dead. The lack of information left him pacing in frustration.

Upon receiving the radio call, Mitch had immediately mobilized the ambulance staff, one of which was always on hand at these events. He directed two of the local club members to guide the crew to the first checkpoint. The ambulance would have to negotiate the maze of jeep trails in this part of the Olustee National Forest. He hoped that they could backtrack to the downed rider and retrieve him before it was too late.

Now he couldn't sit still any longer. Two of his buddies, Paul Wedgefield and Wayne Lenoir, were asking him what they could do to help. "Get your bikes and follow me," he replied, heading for his campsite.

By the time he had put on his riding gear, the others had arrived. "I'm going nuts here," Mitch told them. "We need to find out what happened." He stuffed a two-way radio into his fanny pack, then straddled his machine. He stroked the kickstarter down hard with his right boot. The KTM motorcycle came to life instantly. It surrounded him in a blue haze of exhaust as he gunned the throttle to warm the engine. Disengaging the choke and easing out the clutch, he led the way to the starting line.

The late rows of riders were still leaving at one-minute intervals. Row forty-six had just left. Mitch and his two friends fell in behind. The course was now well marked, with a two foot wide ribbon of freshly turned sand winding through the planted pines.

As Mitch, Paul and Wayne caught up to the other riders one by one, Mitch gave a loud whistle to request a pass. Each of the slower riders let them by. Soon the three were moving quickly down the trail. Concern for the downed rider sucked all the enjoyment from their ride. They didn't know how far they had to go, but they all dreaded what they would find before the first checkpoint.

By the time they reached the end of the clear-cut, a crowd had gathered around the ambulance. Mitch Clanton feared the worst. Only a serious accident would cause this many riders to abandon the race. As they shut down their machines, the silence struck them. Over two-hundred riders were sitting or standing there, but they could have heard a leaf drop.

Mitch watched as a draped figure on a litter was loaded into the ambulance. Only a pair of riding boots stuck out from the sheet. He recognized Mark Jemison's custom-painted helmet next to the medic's bag. It was spattered with blood. Mitch felt like his heart had fallen into his stomach. He swallowed hard.

Sam Braselton had radioed the first account of the accident. He was standing solemnly behind the ambulance, shaking his head and staring at the ground between his feet. He seemed to come out of a trance as Mitch approached and asked him what had happened.

"This is really bad," Sam said. "Mark's been killed."

"What do you mean killed?"

"Someone set a wire across the trail."

The words hit Mitch like a slap in the face. Over the years, the Florida Dirt Riders had lost a few members during races. Mostly they were older riders who fell victim to natural causes like heart attacks. Only one rider had died from an accident, rupturing his spleen. Mitch could in concept accept these things happening. But murder?

"Are you sure it was on purpose?"

"Wait till you see," Sam said, motioning toward the trail on his left.

Mitch turned and walked in that direction, toward the course arrows. As he went, his mind reeled and wandered. Peripheral senses faded away, no longer important. He lost feeling in his feet. He could see his boots hitting the ground, but there was only a numb, distant sensation of impact with the earth. Death's black dog always threw him into this semi-paralysis when it came sniffing too near. At the end of the straightaway were two pines bracketing the trail. As he looked closer, he saw several wraps of wire around each tree, less than five feet above the ground. The wire was pulled deeply into the bark. A loose coil, kinked and broken, hung from the nearest pine.

Ahead was a dark patch in the middle of the trail. He approached it and knelt close to the pool of blood. It had only partially soaked into the sand. Staring blankly at the coagulating mass, his mind wandered back to a lawyer's seminar on blood evidence. It had covered more than everything he wanted to know about blood and DNA. He pictured the reaction of Mark Jemison's living blood when it made contact with the sand; white cells mindlessly searching for microscopic enemies to kill, platelets forming clots to stop the flow. How did the soil organisms react? Did they fight back? Had they already begun to use the hemoglobin as food? Mitch shook himself to regain his senses. He walked to where Mark's motorcycle lay. It had not been damaged in the crash. The front wheel was aiming at the sky. Mitch looked up between the trees. "Godspeed, old buddy," he said quietly. Odd, he thought, how death brings out such statements from infidels like himself. Anything to make it better, less final.

Mitch's instinct was to right the bike, to prevent fuel from draining onto the ground. He reached down, then noticed the spiderwebs across the handlebars. His hand drew back by reflex. He shared Mark's dislike of spiders and their flair for laying webs across trails and waiting, smack in the middle, for lunch. He especially hated it when they got plastered against his goggles. Once he was sure none of the web-spinners were present, he brushed off the handlebars and started to lift the bike. But then he stopped. The police might not want it disturbed.

Turning to walk back, his shock suddenly switched to anger. He ripped a course arrow down, then kicked one of wired trees, sending patches of bark flying. He remembered Mark's girlfriend, Hallie Shugart. She was the state environmental specialist assigned to monitor their races. Mitch had introduced her to Mark and the others at the last awards banquet. She was a natural beauty in her late twenties. The guys were like moths drawn to a flame when they learned she needed assistance with her research. Mitch Clanton would have been interested, except for Melanie, his fiancee. Hallie Shugart had chosen Mark Jemison. Mitch shook his head at the sad twist of fate. He wondered how close the two of them had become and how badly she would take it.

Without warning, his thoughts were shattered by a loud staccato noise erupting overhead. A sheriff's department helicopter banked sharply and sandblasted the gathered riders. It set down a short distance from the ambulance in the clear cut. As Mitch emerged from the woods he stuck his fingers in his ears. A stress headache had started above his eyes. The noise was pushing the pain toward a collision at the center of his forehead. Two men, one tall figure in uniform and one short man in coat and tie, were getting out of the helicopter. They jogged toward the ambulance, bent over at the waist to avoid the propwash. The whine of the jet engine slowly died behind them.

Mitch recognized the non-uniformed man as Charlie Dorge, a local homicide detective. He had met him when one of his more disturbed clients had committed suicide. Mitch found the detective to be an arrogant bully with no compassion. He couldn't forgive the way Dorge had treated the wife of the deceased. Handcuffed to her own refrigerator, she was forced to watch as the police searched and prodded her lifeless husband lying in a pool of blood. Not until the body had been photographed and bagged did Charlie Dorge let her loose. This, without evidence that she was anything but a grieving widow. The disdain that Mitch felt had been mutual, and the two of them had more than once exchanged harsh words. Seeing the detective's familiar furrowed brow and permanent sneer made his mood blacker still. Mitch Clanton rubbed his knuckles hard on his temples and kept walking.

By the time Mitch reached the assembled group of riders, the detective had ordered all of them away from the ambulance. Charlie Dorge wanted to know who was in charge. Mitch knew that whoever stepped forward would be in for a tough time. He also knew that he had to be the one. He brushed back his hair, clenched his jaw, and approached the shorter man. "I guess that would be me," he said.

"Hey, don't I know you?" Dorge said.

"Yes, you might remember me, I'm ..."

"You're the smart guy attorney who doesn't like my bedside manner,"

"What do you want?" Mitch said, feeling his blood pressure rise.

"It seems you dirtfreaks have a possible homicide on your hands. The call from the ambulance said a man had been killed by some kind of snare."

"A local rider named Mark Jemison was the first one on the trail. He ran into a wire that appears to have been deliberately set. It happened down that trail." Mitch pointed back the way he had come.

"Is he in there?" The detective motioned toward the ambulance.

"Yes, but I haven't seem him yet."

"I'll decide who sees what around here, you overpaid shyster," Dorge warned.

Turning to the uniformed deputy, the detective ordered him to secure the scene and take names of possible witnesses. At the back of the ambulance, he picked at his nose, then pointed at one of the attendants.

"Let me have a look at the stiff."

The nearest attendant narrowed his eyes as he looked at the detective. He hated rubberneckers, especially ones with badges.

"What for?"

"I have a fetish for dead guys, that's what for."

The attendant shrugged his shoulders and opened the back door. "Its not very pretty."

Charlie Dorge leaned into the ambulance and pulled aside the sheet. He whistled loudly. "That would ruin your day."

Turning toward Mitch, the detective lowered his designer sunglasses and motioned him to come closer. He looked serious. "Come here, Clanton, I need to ask you something."

Reluctant to see his friend dead, but willing to help if possible, Mitch approached the open door.

"What is it?" he said, keeping his eyes off Mark's nearly severed neck.

"I can't get anything out of him. He's your buddy, ask him who did it."

Mitch shut his eyes and turned away. "Jesus, Dorge...you are a cold blooded son-of-a-bitch".

"And proud of it," the detective laughed as

he flipped down his shades. "Otherwise, I might be some bleeding heart Robin Hood lawyer like you."

Mitch Clanton was within seconds of losing control. The pain in his head flared with every heartbeat. He sorely wanted to see his fist slamming into the detective's jaw. His hands tightened into solid blocks of bone and muscle. Sam Braselton noticed this just in time. He had seen Mitch like this before. He moved in quickly and put his hand on Mitch's shoulder. He could feel the muscles tense with anger.

"The officer needs your help over there," Sam said, pointing toward the woods.

Mitch Clanton gave the detective a long glare, then walked toward the deputy. His fingers slowly uncurled. Then he led the officer to the two pine trees down the bloody trail. Behind them, the ambulance pulled out, slowly, not bothering with the siren or lights.

After assisting the deputy, Mitch and Sam got on their radios to the other checkpoints. They told the crews that the race was being called. It had self-destructed at the ambulance.

By that evening, Mitch was spent. Dealing with the death, the detective and the multitude of questions had drained him. They were no closer to knowing who could have done this, or why, than they were that morning. The crime scene had yielded very little. Even without the disturbance of the riders and the ambulance crew bringing out the body, there was little chance of finding much evidence. Whoever placed the wire had done so quickly and carefully. The pre-rider for this section had seen nothing unusual, nor had the nearby checkpoint crew. Even the slower riders in the same row as Mark Jemison had seen nothing. Nothing, that is, except for him bleeding out his last few ounces of blood. The female rider had tried to stem the flow, but realized it was hopeless and gave up.

Turning onto the shell drive leading to his house, Mitch wondered how he might track down Hallie Shugart. No one had been able to contact her that day. They suspected that she was camped out at her latest research site northwest of Daytona. She was known to get wrapped up in her work and not emerge from the woods for days at a time. She carried a cell phone, but had apparently not turned it on. He would worry about finding her tomorrow.

Mitch Clanton got out of his van and walked toward the darkened house. A lone streetlight illuminated a raccoon trying to get into his garbage cans. It jumped down and ran as he approached. Mitch liked raccoons, just not in his garbage. It had taken a while to develop a system for keeping them out of the cans that he could put up with. The little bandits were very good at getting past most obstacles. Motorcycle tie downs did the trick. Too tough to chew through, but easy to adjust. He checked the straps holding the lids down. Satisfied they were secure, he looked up at the stars. His contemplations were interrupted by a mosquito seeking dinner on the back of his hand. "Not tonight," he said, slapping it with his other hand. As he brushed the remains off, he was struck with the uncomfortable reality that life was indeed fleeting. Dark thoughts swam though his mind. Man or mosquito, what's the difference? He wished he could turn off his brain for a while.

As he went up the front steps, Mitch felt very alone. It had been almost four months since Melanie had left without warning. He told himself it was the her red hair. Temperamental. More likely she grew tired of sharing him with his two-wheeled addiction and riding buddies. Probably better off anyway. Marriage would have only postponed the inevitable split...he knew the statistics. Now Mitch was playing the field again, but nothing good had materialized. He crossed the dining room to his liquor cabinet and searched out the best bourbon he had. He made a Manhattan and went into the living room. Collapsing in his recliner, Mitch hit the remote for the TV. The ten o'clock news should be starting. He wondered what they would say about the homicide.

The local station had picked up the story.

As he washed down some aspirin with the booze, Mitch grimaced to see their glitzy blond live scene reporter basking in the glare of floodlights. The station conducted live "eyewitness" stories wherever a tragedy had happened in their viewing area. They didn't seem to care that by broadcast time their crews were usually the only ones there. That night, the reporter was delivering a monologue on the tragic scene from somewhere out in the woods. The lights were bringing in swarms of insects. One of the bugs managed to fly up her nose during an inhale. Covering the other nostril, she blew it out and kept talking...loudly. The spring peepers were in full voice, and they threatened to drown her out.

"What a circus," Mitch muttered.

The news report shed no new light on the homicide. But it did draw attention to the fact that off-road motorcycling had critics. The reporter implied that environmental extremists might be involved. This had also occurred to the sheriff's department. Mitch had occasionally dealt with the environmental community. Although they were sometimes combative, murder wasn't their style. Not that one of them couldn't have gone off the deep end.

He walked in darkness down the hall to the bathroom. Eyes shut, he flipped on the light and cranked the hot water on. Waiting for it to heat,

Mitch leaned against the sink, slowly opening his eyes and staring at himself in the mirror. It had been some time since he had taken a good look. The brown eyes staring back were clear and intense. He searched for gray along his temples. It relieved him to see only dirty blonde. Wrinkles he didn't remember creased the tanned skin under his eyes. Two days growth of beard shadowed his face. Mitch decided it made him look either rugged or unwashed. "Better shave", he told his reflection.

A hot shower helped wash away some of the day's tension. Toweling off, he massaged the ache beneath the scar on the side of his left knee. A souvenir from high school football. He wished he had thought to put on his knee braces that day. He dripped his way toward the kitchen, pausing to punch up his Blind Faith CD on the stereo. Too tired to fix a proper dinner, he mashed a banana on a whole wheat peanut butter sandwich, then topped it off with walnuts and honey. He wolfed down the sticky mess and chased it with orange juice. It was still early for him, but some extra zees would be welcome.

Falling into bed, he mentally replayed the events of the day and the times he had shared with Mark Jemison. In the late 80's, they were in a group of six riders that entered nearly all the out of state enduros in the Southeast. The camaraderie of traveling in his motorhome had been a high point of

Mitch's riding career. As time went on, careers and marriages got in the way. They finally quit going. It had been over a year since he had socialized with Mark. Just one more piece of his life he couldn't go back to, he thought. He felt ashamed of his self pity as he tried to fall asleep. But an imaginary wire was cutting into his trachea. One hand went to his throat and rubbed off the phantom sensation. A dreamless sleep engulfed him.

CHAPTER III

The day after the Sand Pine Enduro, Hallie Shugart was somewhere on a vast tract of land owned by a major cattle company. She was deep into documenting the ecological conditions before an upcoming race. This time of year the enduros came almost every other weekend, and it was all she could do to keep up with her work. She had been busy all weekend, camping out in the back of her truck, anxious to finish this site. A hot shower and a quiet evening with Mark would suit her fine. They had a few things to iron out, but she was willing to work on their relationship if he was.

She had been both pleased and puzzled by her assignment. After pushing papers for more than eight years in Tallahassee, she was finally getting a chance to use her scientific skills. It had also allowed her to put some distance between herself and a recent ex-boyfriend. Pausing to take a slug of water from her canteen, she thought back to the call from the chairman of the state trails committee. It had come out of the blue. Curious as to why she was chosen, Hallie had investigated the selection. She knew that all public meetings were recorded for posterity. So she had searched out the transcripts from the committee that had hired her.

What she was not able to find out was that Mel Coburn, the chairman of the state Trails Advisory Council, or TAC Group, was having a problem. The federal government was about to turn over several hundred thousand dollars to his council, and he was concerned about how it would be spent. The money was derived from fuel taxes that the federal government had levied. The trouble was, the taxes were a prorated share, representing the amount paid for fueling off-road vehicles. The money was earmarked by the federal government to benefit those who had contributed the funds. Since off-road vehicles did not use paved highways, their money was to be spent on creating and maintaining unpaved trails. That was not the aim of the chairman. Mel was a hunter and horseman to his bones, and the only trails that he intended to promote would be for hunting or horseback riding. Even bicycling he viewed with suspicion.

The TAC Group had been formed to assure that public lands, paid for by the taxpayers of Florida, would be open to recreation. The makeup of the Council had been left to the Department of Environmental Control. They had appointed Coburn, a former sugar industry lobbyist, to lead the group. His name had been suggested by a state senator as payback for funneling political contributions to his election campaign. The department had gone along with the suggestion, confident that the senator would keep his promise to sponsor an environmental bill or two during the next legislative session. Mel had been able to get a few of his cronies added to the council, but most of the members did not take the committee as seriously as the chairman.

Mel Coburn had, over the previous two years, managed to bring the council under his complete control by secretly encouraging the environmental community to lobby the committee for favors. He would always step in and mediate the pre-arranged solution. This earned him the gratitude and votes of the other council members. They liked having Mel standing as a shield between themselves and the "greenies", so they gave him free rein.

Under his guidance, the Council had moved steadily toward prohibiting motorized use of any kind on "their" land. But the new federal tax money would make it harder to pursue that agenda. The chairman's first reaction had been to keep the federal money a secret. He ignored the very groups that it was intended to benefit. This strategy unraveled when an article appeared in a major newspaper, telling of the money and how it was supposed to be spent. Mel Coburn backpedaled skillfully to avoid any blame for mismanaging the money. He pulled it off without breaking a sweat. But he had no intention of changing direction.

On a midweek afternoon in September, purposely chosen to discourage attendance, the council had reluctantly received testimony from Mitch Clanton on behalf of FDRA. Mitch was well aware of the leanings of his group. He hoped he would not have to threaten legal action to get them to follow the federal guidelines for the money. Hallie had found the transcript of this hearing.

On that day, the chairman was asking the questions:

"Just what sort of motorcycle races does your club sanction on public lands, Mr. Clanton?"

"Our association sanctions enduros on both public and private lands."

"Could you explain to the Council what an enduro is, please?"

"An enduro is a motorcycle endurance event in which the competitors try to maintain a pre-set schedule and speed on a marked course through off-road terrain." Mitch continued, "in the strictest sense, an enduro is a timed event, not a race."

"What is the point of these races, Mr. Clanton?"

"Well, mainly to have fun, but the

association awards trophies to riders who finish in the top three or four positions in each class, so there is a competitive side to it."

"How many riders compete in these races?"

"FDRA has over two thousand members, and there are thousands of additional riders in out of state organizations that can come to our events. The average enduro draws about three to four hundred riders."

"That many?" The chairman gave Mitch a skeptical look.

"Yes. In fact there is one enduro that draws five hundred riders from all over the world, year after year. That particular event could probably draw twice as many entries, but they have to cut it off. Otherwise, they'd be out in the woods until midnight."

The chairman continued. "So you put five hundred riders into the woods at one time. Doesn't that do quite a bit of damage?"

Mitch sensed that the chairman was trying for a quick kill. He knew that his response could have tremendous impact on his sport, so he could not afford to stray from the absolute truth.

"The course is laid out using arrow cards on a single trail. Much of the time the trail is an existing firebreak, logging road or hunting trail. Planted pine forests, clear-cuts and smaller trails are also used. In natural terrain, the disturbance is generally limited to a very narrow path of about two to three feet or so. The riders are sent out five at a time at one-minute intervals. It's all single file riding."

"What about the animals?" interjected a woman council member.

"Well, I've never heard of any being struck during an event. They seem to just move away until the riders pass by."

"What evidence do you have to make that assertion?" She continued to press her point.

"The clean-up crews often see fresh animal tracks on the trails right after an event. Sometimes we'll see a deer standing just a few yards from the trail, watching us go by."

"What are the clean-up crews cleaning up?" the chairman broke in, thinking he had found an opening.

"They go out and take down all the course arrows after the event. They also assist any rider who may have broken down or run out of gas. The same volunteers generally are the ones that lay out the course and pre-ride each section the morning of the event."

"That's all very interesting. But we need to know why you think these races belong on public lands".

Mitch took a long breath as he thought about his response. He adjusted the microphone in front of him, then began, "As I stated, these events take place on both public and private lands. It requires at least three or four thousand acres to lay out a decent fifty to seventy mile course. The government has been buying up the large undeveloped parcels at a steady pace. Now we don't have much choice except to use public lands. I should also note that these events have been taking place all around Florida for about fifty years. Many of the highly prized public acquisition areas have been the site of enduros. So even in very sensitive areas there appears to have been little or no impact from our sport."

The chairman was getting impatient. "Let's change the subject, then. What else does your organization do?"

"Well, besides promoting all types of off-road motorcycling, we also support local charities and fund scholarships. When some state or federal park needs help with trails, we have members who will volunteer to work."

The chairman was visibly frustrated. "What is it you think this Council can do for your organization?"

"We propose that part of the fuel tax money should go to developing and maintaining a more organized trail system for off-road vehicles. There is currently little order to the trail areas, and recreational riding is becoming more and more popular. If an interconnected trail system can be created, it could serve both competition and casual use. We also believe that an organized trail system would be safer and environmentally compatible. Maintained, marked trails would discourage riders from making their own trails. Also, FDRA would be willing to assist in locating and maintaining these trails, saving taxpayer dollars."

The transcript continued, with neither side gaining nor losing ground. The TAC Group still lacked good reasons for limiting or excluding motorized vehicles from the trails program. Coburn knew that environmentalists had always been quick to condemn the use of off-road vehicles. But a lot of the evidence they used was from very sensitive areas that were subject to year round intense use by large off-road vehicles. Managed trails were another matter, and there were no scientific studies to show that this sort of off-road recreation was any more harmful to the ecology of Florida than non-motorized recreation. The Council decided that they needed to commission a study. To their surprise, the FDRA president endorsed this idea. He even offered the services of his organization to assist in the research.

After the public meeting, the TAC Group met in private at a local pub. They agreed to find a dedicated ecologist who would go forth and prove them right...one with enough credentials to be believable. But it had to be an insider who would not be sympathetic to the off-roaders. Because they did not want to spend committee funds on the project, the researcher would be someone who already worked for the state.

Over the next few months they had searched the ranks of agency employees for the right person. Hallie Shugart's name rose to the top of the heap. She had a master's degree in vertebrate zoology and was a competent botanist. As a senior permit reviewer with the Florida Department of Environmental Control, she had become known as a knowledgeable, no-nonsense scientist who could hammer stubborn developers into submission or tie them in knots at hearings. Coburn felt satisfied that she would be perfect for infiltrating the largest off-road user group in the state. He told the other committee members that she was just the ticket to build a case against the dirt bikers and anyone else who didn't share the committee member's interests. Besides, he thought to himself, she's a looker and you never know when you're going to get lucky. None of this made it to the public record.

Although she suspected that her selection was intended to serve the TAC agenda, Hallie considered the assignment a welcome break. The new working hours were unpredictable and the conditions were sometimes difficult, but she liked being outdoors. And the riders treated her well...

one in particular. In any case, this two-year study was better than the tedium of reviewing the endless flow of new development permits.

Since starting the study, Hallie had already researched and documented the habitats and wildlife patterns of several race sites, including the Olustee National Forest at the Sand Pine Enduro. She would re-evaluate her study areas after the races to determine what changes had occurred. Additional studies would be conducted about one year later. Then she could quantify and qualify the impacts. So far, her work had gathered substantial data, but it was too early to draw any conclusions.

Today, she was laying out vegetation sampling transects through a large forest of planted pines. Although guided by widely-spaced orange ribbons tied to trees by the course layout crew, she was having trouble staying on track. The local club was using the same trail as the previous year, but there was little evidence of the old course. Pine needles, grasses and shrubs had obscured the path. She found herself resorting to a careful inspection of the trees for any telltale rusted staples that held up last year's arrow cards.

Satisfied once more that she was in the right place, Hallie Shugart screwed the cap back on the canteen and drove a wooden stake in the ground. She pulled a compass from the top of her blouse by the lanyard. Sighting on a distant tree, she headed due east along the course. As her hip chain kept track of the distance from the stake, she placed pin flags at ten meter intervals. Later, she would nail numbered aluminum disks to the trees nearest each pin flag. At each point she took a photograph and recorded the species of plants that grew there. The final step was to remove the pin flags and stakes. She could re-establish all the sampling points by using the numbered trees and her field notes.

It was tedious work, but it was the only way to assure scientifically valid results. Sometimes, Mark Jemison would take time off work to assist her. But this was the day after an enduro, so she knew just making it out of bed before noon would be a stretch for him.

After finishing the transect, she headed back toward her four-wheel-drive pickup. As she stepped across the shallow ditch along the dirt road, a juvenile brown water snake darted into a clump of submerged grass. Its nostrils popped up, just barely protruding from the water. Hallie recognized the species as harmless. She slowly stooped down, then quickly grabbed for it, getting both snake and grass between her fingers.

She gently held it up for a closer look. After first trying to squirm from her grasp, the snake calmed down and let itself be examined.

Hallie did not advertise a certain fact: She had a fascination for snakes. She had learned a lot about them over the years. This understanding had been encouraged by her father, who always taught her not to be afraid of nature. Every time she looked closely at a snake, she remembered the first time he held one up for her inspection. It was a small garter snake. He had found it in their rock garden in suburban Illinois. She was only three years old at the time, and was thrilled when he let her hold it. The creature was the most amazing toy she had ever seen. The iridescent green and brown scales were etched with rainbow colors in the sunlight. And the unblinking eyes, they seemed to look deep into her, taking in everything as its forked tongue softly tickled her nose. She could still remember his instructions not to squeeze the small, frightened animal. Thinking about it, she felt a lump rise in her throat. Her father was no longer there to teach her, and she missed him terribly.

Placing the snake back in the water, she washed the musky odor of the animal from her hand and walked to her vehicle. After making a few final notes, she started up and headed toward her next sampling site.

Hallie noticed that she had forgotten to turn on her cell phone. She hit the power button and called Mark's apartment. Puzzled that she got no answer, she felt slightly concerned. Her efforts to call him the night before had also failed. But she knew Mark could sleep very soundly after a race.

CHAPTER IV

As she was opening the gate at a cross fence on the property, Hallie heard the cell phone ring. Thinking it was Mark, she hurried back to the truck and punched the receive button, saying, "Haven't I told you not to call me at work?"

The voice at the other end was familiar, but not who she had expected.

"Is this Hallie?"

"Yeah, who's this?"

"Mitch Clanton."

"I thought I recognized your voice...what's up?"

"Listen Hallie, something's happened." Mitch thought for a moment that the connection had been broken. "You still there?" he asked.

"It's Mark, isn't it?" Hallie felt fear rising in her chest as she spoke. "He's okay, isn't he?"

"Where are you?"

"What's happened?" she insisted, feeling her hands go cold against the gray plastic of the cellular.

"I want to come and get you...where are you?" Mitch got no reply, then he heard her voice rise as she spit out her words.

"You have to tell me....is Mark okay?"

"Hallie, please tell me where you are."

She had to work to wet her lips. "Not till you level with me," she said with finality.

Mitch realized he had trapped himself. He had wanted to tell her in person. But now he couldn't keep the truth from her. "No, Hallie, I'm so sorry...he's not okay...."

By the time Mitch had arrived at her study site, Hallie was nearly cried out. She sat thirty feet from the dirt road with her back against a large pine. Her head was upright, resting on the tree. Behind her sunglasses, her eyes were shut. As Mitch parked his van and walked toward her, she did not open them.

"Why did this happen?" she said abruptly when he was close by.

"Nobody knows...the police are working on it"

"Who would want to hurt him?"

"He was on the first row, it would have happened to whoever was up front." Mitch winced, knowing this explanation was less than comforting.

He moved to the side of the tree and sat beside her. "I don't know what this world is

36

coming to..."

Hallie sniffed and pulled at a strand of her long blond hair. Mitch could think of nothing to say to ease her pain. Not knowing what else to do, he took her hand and squeezed it gently.

"Mark had a lot of friends...we're all going to miss him."

Hallie opened her eyes slightly. "It feels like this should just be a bad dream...I want to wake up and find this never really happened."

"I wish we could all do that."

"But it's not going to happen," she said, rolling her head slowly from side to side.

"No, I'm afraid it's not."

After a silence, Hallie asked, "Where is he?"

"At the county coroner's in Daytona."

"I want to see him."

"Of course," Mitch said quietly.

"Does his family know?"

"Yes, his father is flying back today from a fishing trip in the Bahamas...his mom is driving up from Sarasota."

"What happens now?"

"Well, the detective in charge of the case wants to ask you and a few of the riders some questions."

"Why?"

"He has some theories about what might have happened and thinks you might be able to fill in some missing pieces."

"I don't think I'm going to be any help."

"You never know. Maybe he's just looking to know who Mark had been hanging around with."

"Nobody I know could have had anything to do with this...do I have to talk to him?"

"I'm afraid so. But I should warn you, the detective is a total jerk. His name is Charlie Dorge and you won't get any sympathy from him."

"Swell."

"Would you like someone there for moral support?"

"That would be good...keep me off his suspect list. You are an attorney, right?"

Mitch was glad to see Hallie start to come out of her state of despair. So far, he was impressed by her reserve and self control. Some people would have gone to pieces. He tried to think of how he would have felt had his fiancee met an untimely end. Her sudden voluntary departure, however, had tainted his memory of her.

"I need to get cleaned up before I go into town," Hallie said, wiping tear stains from her face.

"No big hurry. Anyway, you can drop your truck off at your apartment and I'll drive you in."

As he helped her to her feet, Mitch was surprised at her strength. It was no wonder that she had quickly learned to ride a dirt bike with Mark's help.

He arranged to meet Hallie later that afternoon. He needed to stop by the Olustee Forest to talk to the local members of the Daytona Sand Slingers. Some of them would be riding cleanup for the aborted Sand Pine Enduro. He wanted to deliver a request from the homicide detective and get their input on the next race. It was the grandad of Florida enduros, known worldwide as simply "The Alligator". Since Daytona was the sponsoring club, he wanted to know how they were going to deal with the recent events.

CHAPTER V

The Alligator has been run for the past half century without fail. The phenomenal popularity of the race is due in part to the fact that it is held during Bike Week. For ten days each spring, almost every form of motorcycle competition on earth can be found within a short distance of Daytona. Road racing is the main event, but oval dirt track, motocross, drag racing, hare scrambles, dual sport and The Alligator rounded out the menu. If they could get a lake to freeze in Florida, there would likely be ice racing as well. Riders and spectators flock there from all over the world.

A hotly contested event, The Alligator attracts the best off-road competitors each year. The cream of the crop are factory supported riders, since the bragging rights are worth a year of good dirt bike sales to the winning brand. Taking points from riders of that caliber is tough, so the event is purposely difficult, but not impossible. Lesser competitors, not used to such tight trails and bottomless mud holes, are often disqualified by being more than sixty minutes late to one of the eight or nine checkpoints.

Putting on an enduro is a daunting task. First there is the question of land availability, then legal and logistical arrangements. But most of all there's the layout work. It takes at least a dozen volunteers four or five weekends to choose the trails, put up arrow cards, mileage the course and find good places for checkpoints and the gas stops. The paperwork is also formidable, so it is shared by all the members of the sponsoring club.

The Alligator was only ten days away. Mitch Clanton knew that the news of the murder would sweep through the motorcycling community long before the event. He hoped the sponsoring club was ready.

Pulling into the Olustee campground, he looked around for riders. Several vehicles were parked in the shade under the live oaks, but no one was in sight. Mitch pulled alongside Paul Wedgefield's pickup. He lowered the driver's side window and waited for the cleanup crew to show. As he sat there, he wondered about the fate of this sport. It just kept getting tougher each year. How much public lands would stay open to multiple uses? It was acceptable in this day and age. But what about a century from now, or two? Would they be locked out of all public lands? Worse yet, would there be a backlash against preservation, with the government selling off the once precious resources? He hoped that things would not change. A big part of the reason they raced was to enjoy the outdoors. Without the woods, there could be no enduros. Mitch mused over this, then started planning a fishing trip in the back of his mind. Finally, in the distance, he heard the sound of several dirt bikes approaching.

Three riders appeared from the woods at the far end of the campground. He recognized them as Paul Wedgefield and Sam Braselton, with Rusty McInster bringing up the rear.

Sam had been a lightning quick rider in his younger days. He didn't take the competition as seriously any more, but he still loved to ride. Short and agile, Sam was always up to a challenge. Mitch and Sam had gone to high school together, and learned to ride on an old motorcycle they bought at a junkyard and patched up. Paul Wedgefield had been two grades above them. He was one of the few upper classmen who would be caught dead with freshmen and sophomores. Anyone who would ride in the woods on weekends was old enough for Paul. He wasn't the best rider, but he was tireless and enthusiastic to a fault. No matter how tough the trails got, he would find something to enjoy about it.

Mitch didn't know Rusty McInster very well. They said the thin redhead had drifted down from Alabama, joining the Sand Slingers a year ago. Mitch had heard that he was related to half the population of Possum Bluff, a rural community scattered along the east bank of the St. Johns River. Rumor had it that the town's entire gene pool wouldn't fill a shot glass. For whatever reason, Rusty was reluctant to discuss his many cousins.

The three riders pulled up near the parked vehicles and took off their helmets. The temperature had climbed into the upper eighties. The dust on their faces was turning to sweat streaked mud. Mitch held Paul's bike while he retrieved the cycle stand from the back of his pickup.

"Want a drink?" Paul asked Mitch as he flipped open the lid of his cooler and tossed a dripping wet can at Mitch's chest.

"Sure." Mitch caught it deftly with his free hand.

After securing Paul's bike, Mitch and the three riders sat under the oaks, out of the hot sun. The riders passed around a wet towel to wipe off their faces.

"How's it going with cleanup?"

"Pretty good," Sam volunteered. "Rusty's bike has been acting up, but we got the first half and most of the second loop taken down."

Mitch turned to Rusty. "What's wrong with

your bike?"

"I think I got some bad gas last week at the mini-mart...it hasn't been running good since then."

"Why don't you get some fresh fuel?"

"I didn't know what to do with the old stuff...couldn't just waste it".

"Shoot, sell it to Paul, his truck will run on sludge".

Paul gave Mitch a dirty look. "You cockroach, quit making fun of Old Blue...he may be old, but he runs great."

"Oh sure, Paul," Sam interjected. "You not only get where you're going, you fog for mosquitos at the same time. The county should be paying you to drive around. Besides, your truck's red, not blue."

"It's my truck and I can call it anything I want...and if I want to be abused, I'll go hunt up my ex." Paul snapped back.

Mitch hated to end the friendly jabbing he had started, but there was serious business to discuss.

"You guys didn't see anything out of the ordinary, especially on the first leg?"

"Nope," Paul said. "The cops have yellow ribbon up around where Mark went down, so we stayed away from there."

"Any cops out there now?"

"A couple were here earlier. They took off

about an hour ago."

"The detective called me first thing this morning and asked if I'd follow up on some of the information he's after. In particular, Rusty, he wants to ask you about the pre-ride of the first section again. He thinks there may be some detail you might have remembered since yesterday."

"I told him all I know already." Rusty whined. "That Dorge guy is a real drag...he thinks people have photomatic memories or something."

"You mean photographic."

"Whatever, he makes me nervous, that's all."

"I don't know anyone who likes dealing with him," Mitch said. "But he's in charge of the case and we need to help him any way we can. I'm going to the station myself this afternoon ...maybe you could meet me there."

"Can't I go in some other time?...We still have some trail to sweep...I want to do my share of the work."

"I think Dorge might have a problem with that. I'm taking Hallie Shugart to see him later today. He wants to ask her some questions too."

"You found Hallie?"

"Yeah, she was out at the Alligator site."

"How'd she take it?" asked Sam.

"She's having a rough time of it, but seems to be holding up pretty well."

"Is she going back to Tallahassee?" asked Rusty.

"She didn't mention it...why?"

"No reason," Rusty answered defensively.

"Right now she just needs to sort things out, so let's give her some room." Mitch steadied his gaze on Rusty. "Well, did you decide if you're going to the station with us?"

"Oh, alright... I'll be there."

Mitch turned to Sam and Paul. "You guys are pretty close to finishing the layout for The Alligator, aren't you?"

"We got it all laid out," said Sam. "Joe Brown's trail boss again, so we've been bustin' ass the last few weeks. Once we're done here we need to get over there and finish the arrowing."

"Have you thought about security...I mean, since this happened?"

"We're worried sick about it. It'll be the main topic at the next meeting on Wednesday night for sure. The club's going to need some help to keep things together. You might want to come and discuss it," Paul suggested.

Mitch thought for a moment. "I guess it's about time I made the rounds."

Mitch said his goodbyes and headed to Hallie's apartment. When he arrived, she was outside, pacing across the commons in front of her building. Her hair was wet, and she was holding a bright orange and black placard in one hand. She hurried to his van as he pulled up.

"Look at this!" she said as Mitch opened the door. Mitch immediately recognized the enduro course arrow.

"Someone stapled this to my front door when I was getting cleaned up....look at the back".

Mitch took the arrow card and turned it over. On the back, in a mix of print and crude cursive, was the message:

NOW YOUR FREE AS A BIRD SHUGAR
DON'T MAKE ANUTHER MISTAKE

Mitch exhaled slowly and audibly, trying to make sense of this unexpected turn of events. It was obvious that the fate of Mark Jemison was not a random act of violence. Whoever committed the crime had a motive, and it involved Hallie. Mitch was now concerned for her safety, but he did not want to overreact.

"Let's get over to the Sheriff's department. They need to see this right away."

He carefully placed the message in his briefcase and opened the passenger door for her. On the way to see Charlie Dorge, Mitch learned from Hallie that she was getting dressed when she heard two sharp raps on her front door. Thinking it was Mitch, she threw on a robe and opened the

47

door. But nobody was there, just the arrow card. Whoever the culprit was, they had left in a hurry.

Pulling into the parking lot of the Sheriff's department, Mitch was relieved to have avoided the coroner's office for now. The thought of seeing his friend's body again was bad enough, but with Hallie along he knew it was going to be a more painful experience.

As they checked in with the desk sergeant, Mitch was surprised to see Rusty McInster already being questioned by Charlie Dorge and another plainclothes officer in an adjacent room.

Rusty still wore his riding pants and jersey, with only socks on his feet. He appeared quite agitated. Mitch motioned Hallie to stay with the desk sergeant as he moved closer to the interrogation room to check things out.

Through the thick glass, Mitch could not make out the question being directed at Rusty. The reply, however, was easy to hear.

"You're crazy! I never hurt anyone in my whole life!"

Rusty stood up suddenly and tried to leave the room, but he found the door locked. Looking out, he saw Mitch for the first time and waved at him to come in. Mitch tapped on the glass. After some hesitation, Dorge punched numbers into the coded door lock and let him in.

Ignoring the officers, Mitch turned to

Rusty. "Have they accused you of anything?"

"They think I had something to do with Mark's getting killed."

Mitch knew that the arrow card in his briefcase could help exonerate Rusty, since he could not have put it on Hallie's door. He also reasoned that Dorge was on a fishing expedition, but he wanted to know what had led him to Rusty.

"Did they advise you of your right to have an attorney present?"

"This is none of your business, Clanton," Dorge cut in.

"I'm making it my business, Charlie, and if you've been lax on procedure, I'll see that you regret it!"

He repeated his question to Rusty.

"I guess they did, but I told them I don't need one."

"Well, you've got one now, Rusty....OK?"

"Yeah, sure...I guess, but I don't have money for..."

"Don't worry about that. Let's see if we can sort this out. Perhaps the detectives can tell me why they think you're involved."

The officer next to Dorge shrugged his shoulders, then offered Mitch a clear plastic evidence bag. In it was a short piece of braided wire.

"What's this supposed to prove?" Mitch

asked.

"That is a sample of the wire that was used in the homicide," the detective noted. "It's not a very common brand of stainless cable, and your friend here recently bought a large quantity of it."

"I already told them it was for protecting brake and shift levers on the dirt bikes we service at our shop. Everybody who rides in the woods wants them put on."

"It isn't legitimate uses that we're concerned about," the detective continued. "You bought and stored a sizeable spool of this stuff in your shop, but it seems to have disappeared."

"I don't know what happened to it...I'm not the only one who uses it."

"That may be, but you're the only one who was on that first section of trail the morning of the race," Dorge added.

"Is that all you have to go on?" Mitch asked.

"That and a possible motive."

"Such as?"

"Well, it seems your...client here was a little bent out of shape about a certain Hallie Shugart's choice of a boyfriend. We have witnesses who frequent a local watering hole who can testify that he was downright hostile about being turned down by her when she first came to town. Seems he made it known that he wanted to steal her away from one

Mark Jemison, by force if necessary. You may recognize the name of the deceased." The detective was beginning to enjoy himself.

"And I already told him it was just too many beers talking. Sure I wanted her, any man would, but I wouldn't kill anyone to get her."

Mitch felt that he had let this go far enough. He unlatched his briefcase and pulled out the arrow card. "Well, add this to your list of evidence, then."

"What for?" Dorge asked.

Mitch turned it over to show him the message. "Hallie Shugart found this stapled to her front door today."

"The girlfriend, huh...where is she?"

"Out by the desk sergeant."

Dorge turned to the other detective. "Get her in here."

While the other officer fetched her, Mitch tried to reason with the detective. "Take it easy on her, okay? She's been through a lot today."

The detective gave him an insincere smile. "You know me, Mitch, treat everyone the same."

Mitch glowered back. "That's what I'm afraid of."

When Hallie came in, she was motioned to a chair near the center of the room. Dorge moved in front of her, turning the arrow card over slowly in his hands. He looked her up and down, chewing on his lip in contemplation of where to start. The furrows on his forehead deepened. Hallie kept her eyes steadily on his.

"So, they call you Sugar?" he began.

"Not if I can help it," she shot back.

"Okay, then we'll be more formal....Miss Shugart. Do you know this man?" he said, pointing at Rusty McInster.

"Yes, I know Rusty."

"How do you know him?"

"He rides enduros, he's a member of a local motorcycle club."

"You ever go out with him?"

"No."

"Did he ever ask you out?"

"Yeah, I suppose."

"More than once?"

"Maybe."

"This note you found....when did you find it?"

"Around two o'clock this afternoon. I heard a noise at my door and found this card. Whoever stuck it there was gone."

"Do you have any idea who might have done it?"

"No."

"Do you know who might have been out to harm you or Mark Jemison?"

"No."

"You haven't received any threats or

strange calls?"

"No."

"You been flirting around with anybody besides your boyfriend?"

"No," she said sternly.

"Well, were you two lovebirds having a spat?"

Hallie's eyes suddenly flashed with anger. She lunged from her chair at the detective. Dorge saw her fist coming. He managed to catch it two inches from his face. He did not have the same luck with her knee, which she buried in his groin.

Mitch leaped forward and wrapped his arms around Hallie before she could get in another blow. He thought Dorge might retaliate, so he spun around, putting himself between her and the detective.

The detective was doubled over, hands on knees. In a strained voice he said, "I ought to lock you up, you little bitch."

"Don't even think about it," Mitch warned. "Unless you want every uniform in this precinct to know you got beat up by a girl." He hoped the detective's ego would keep this from going any further.

Getting no reaction, Mitch knew it was time to end the interview. "Are you charging my client?" Mitch asked.

Dorge's face reddened. He had not

expected the latest turn of events. Unless he could prove a connection between Rusty and the message, he knew he couldn't hold him.

"Not yet," he answered, beginning to straighten up. "But I want a handwriting sample before he leaves. That okay with you?"

"No problem," Mitch said, turning to Rusty. "Why don't you have any shoes on?"

"These guys picked me up before I could go home and change clothes. They didn't want me wearing my muddy boots in here."

"You need a lift back to your truck?"

"Yeah, I don't want to sit in the back of a squad car again....it made me feel like a criminal."

"If the boot fits," Dorge insinuated. "And by the way, I'd also like to run a polygraph on this character."

Mitch finished ushering Rusty and Hallie out of the room. The sooner he got them out, the more likely to avoid another eruption. He turned to the detective and gave him a noncommittal look. "I'll take that under advisement and let you know."

He had hoped to ask Dorge if he would assign a deputy to watch Hallie for a while. He figured it was futile now, but he had to be sure.

"Detective...someone should keep an eye on Ms. Shugart...do you have a deputy to spare?"

"With Bike Week starting in two days?" Dorge laughed. "We've got every available deputy on overtime just dealing with the early arrivals. Besides, she's tough enough to take care of herself, isn't she?"

"Thanks for nothing, detective."

"Any time."

After leaving a handwriting sample, they collected Rusty's boots and left for the coroner's office. There was an awkward silence to the trip. No one felt like talking. Rusty waited in the van while the other two went in to see Mark.

The coroner's assistant was sympathetic. He carefully arranged a drape on the body to avoid having Hallie see the wicked wound.

She had been through this before. Five years earlier, her mother had been killed by a drunken driver. She and Mitch stood silently next to Mark for a few minutes. Hallie finally reached over and brushed the hair back from his pale forehead. Mitch could see tears glistening on her cheeks. She turned toward him, buried her face against his chest and held on tightly. "Let's go," she whispered. Mitch kept his arm around her as they left the building.

"Let's get Rusty back to his truck," Mitch said as they crossed the parking lot.

"Do you think he had anything to do with it?" she sniffed.

"I don't think so. I don't know him very well, but he seems like a normal guy. Most enduro riders feel a kinship with each other. It's hard for me to believe that any rider would do this to another rider. Besides, he couldn't have left the note on your door."

"I guess you're right. I just feel that I'm missing something. Whoever killed Mark apparently knew me....but I can't make the connection."

"You don't know that for sure. It could be a diversion. Whoever wrote that message seems pretty short on education. You don't know anyone who fits that bill, do you?"

"Not that I can think of."

"Well, if anyone comes to mind, let me know."

On the trip back toward the Olustee campground, Mitch engaged Rusty in conversation, trying to put to rest any concerns about him. He didn't learn much. Finally, he asked a more pointed question.

"Do you want to take a lie-detector test?"

"Do I have to?"

"No, but it could help get the sheriff's department off your back."

"I don't want to take any test."

"Why not?"

"They might trick me into saying something that would make me look like a liar. That could happen, couldn't it?"

"Polygraph tests can be tricky. And they have been known to be interpreted wrong."

"No way, then."

"Okay, if you're sure about that."

"I'm real sure."

Mitch dropped Rusty off at his truck. Before leaving, he pulled Rusty aside and instructed him on dealing with the investigation.

"Whatever you do, Rusty, make sure you let me know before you answer any more questions."

"Okay. Hey, Mitch...you don't think I wanted him dead, do you?"

"I believe you, but I don't think Dorge is ready to give up yet. So don't do anything that would make him suspicious...you know, like leaving town."

"I'm not going nowhere."

"Good. Here's my phone number, stay in touch with me."

"Yeah, sure"

They dropped Rusty off, then Mitch drove Hallie to her apartment. The sun was starting to fade. Mitch felt uneasy leaving her.

"Look, Hallie, you need to be really careful until this is over. Are there any friends in town that you can stay with for a while?"

She turned her puffy eyes downward. "Not any more."

"I just don't feel good about you being alone."

"What are you suggesting?"

"Well, I've got a motorhome I could stay in if you used my house."

"I couldn't impose on you like that."

"It's no imposition, the motorhome is quite comfortable."

"Give me some time to think about it. Everything is just...happening so fast."

"Okay. But in the meantime make sure you keep your doors and windows locked." Mitch thought for a moment. "Didn't Mark get a dog a while back?"

"Yes, he rescued a white German shepherd from the pound...named him White Fang. I could bring him here to stay. He's a good watchdog...and I could use the company."

"Good...do that. And let me know if you need anything."

"I will...thanks....for everything."

"Glad I could help. Are you sure you're going to be okay?"

"I think so. Anyway, I've got some pills I can take...they'll knock me out if I need it."

"Please be careful."

"I will."

"And make sure you get the dog this evening."

"Yes...sir," she added.

Mitch waited down the street until he saw her leave to get White Fang before he drove away.

CHAPTER VI

The next few days brought no new revelations. The handwriting sample from Rusty McInster was inconclusive. No arrests were made. Mark Jemison's remains were laid to rest. His ashes were scattered off the Ponce Inlet jetty on an outgoing tide. He used to surf at the inlet when the waves were good.

The outdoor funeral was attended by over a hundred fellow dirt bikers and surfing buddies. Mitch Clanton and a few of the others delivered short eulogies for their departed friend. Hallie Shugart listened from a distance, staring out over the ocean. Mark's great uncle had shown up with his bagpipes. During the procession to the jetty, he played Amazing Grace. It was about the only song he could still play, what with his arthritis, but he played it well. Even the toughest men wept.

Mitch had taken a couple of weeks off so that he could keep up with the investigation and the Alligator Enduro. He checked on Hallie every day and had met her twice for lunch. He talked her into a movie to provide a diversion from her thoughts and work. She had buried herself in writing up the early findings of her research. A draft report was sent to the TAC group for review.

Meanwhile, Bike Week was in full swing. Over half a million bikers had descended on Daytona. The place was packed. Many years ago, the bikers that showed up were mostly outlaws. Now the thundering Harleys and Harley look-alikes were mainstream. The riders came from all walks of life. White collar professionals on chromed choppers used the occasion to let off steam and temporarily lose themselves for a while. The commercialization of Bike Week had robbed it of some authenticity, but it served its new purpose very well. The local business groups loved the money it brought to town. At least the racing events were still the real thing.

As a teenager, Mitch Clanton had been crazy about Bike Week. He used to camp at the central raceway with his friends. They even managed to sneak their bikes onto the motocross track that was constructed in the infield. Now he was indifferent to all the hoopla, though he did find the changes occasionally amusing. Even the most sacred of the outlaw biker rituals, nude female mud wrestling, had been taken over by the new culture. It was still held in the nearby town of Samsula, but the mud had turned into more civilized coleslaw.

The women who took part still delivered a crowd pleasing spectacle, but they were mostly paid performers, not biker chicks like in the past. The cops looked the other way. Even the local newspaper carried a wrestling schedule.

Two days after the funeral, Mitch was shocked when Hallie called and asked him to take her to see the wrestling.

"You're kidding, right?"

"No, really, I want to see the coleslaw thing."

"What on earth for?"

"I want to see if it's real or not."

"I'm pretty sure it's real...can't you take my word on it?"

"Did you ever go?"

"Well...no."

"Then you're no authority."

"What's so interesting about naked women in coleslaw?" Mitch immediately realized the idiocy of his question. "I mean, to you?"

"I need to go somewhere insane, the more repulsive the better."

"Not you too...there's already enough people like that in town."

"Take me there or I'll go by myself."

"Oh, what the hell, sure...If you insist."

"You'll see, it'll be good for you too."

"Yeah...but I'll never feel the same about

cabbage again."

Mitch stopped by Hallie's place to pick her up for the trip to Samsula. He had dusted off his old BMW motorcycle for the trip. When Hallie saw the vintage machine, she was delighted. Mitch handed her a helmet. "We might as well look the part."

"You're not such a stick in the mud after all," she teased.

Mitch had purposely been trying not to think of Hallie as a possible romantic companion. It hadn't been easy. Ever since he first saw her, he was interested. The perfect complexion, athletic body and...those eyes. Soft blue gray, but outlined in black. Family trait, she had said. Perceptive and piercing. She could take tissue samples with those eyes. Now that he knew her better, it was even harder for him. He found her to have a deliciously dry wit and sharp mind. If Mitch was any judge, the attraction was mutual. But he felt that going further with their relationship at this point would be taking advantage. So he had kept some distance between them. But today she was wearing tight jeans, a low-necked tee shirt and denim vest. He couldn't help noticing she was braless. For Mitch, not reacting to the way she looked was like trying to give up breathing.

When she slid onto the seat behind him and laced her fingers across his stomach, he suddenly wanted her more than life itself.

As they motored away from Daytona, Mitch took some back roads that were not heavily used. When they were off the main highway, Hallie squeezed him and shouted "Faster."

Mitch rolled the throttle and the bike came to life. Nine-hundred cubic centimeters of German engineered muscle carried them effortlessly. At a series of curves, Mitch leaned the bike over hard. Hallie closed her eyes and leaned with the machine. She could feel each shadow they crossed as a momentary coolness on her skin. It was a lot better than a carnival ride.

As they approached Samsula, the traffic picked up. Cars were parked for half a mile along the highway leading to the wrestling grounds. Hundreds of motorcycles were in the parking area. Mitch pulled in and found a spot just vacated by another bike. They could see the overflowing bleachers at the other end of the property. A match was going to start soon.

As they walked toward the coleslaw pit, Mitch felt a little self conscious. Hallie was turning quite a few heads in their direction.

"Oh, Mitch, I forgot to tell you, Rusty called me."

Mitch slowed slightly, mulling over this unwelcome intrusion.

"He did?"

"Yeah, he asked me out."

Mitch watched Hallie out of the corner of his eye, trying to get a read on the situation.

"Sure is persistent," he said.

"Definitely not my kind of guy. And he sounded kind of strange."

"What did you say to him?"

"I told him I was seeing someone," She smiled at Mitch.

"Glad I'm good for something," he said, almost giddily. "How'd he take it?"

"I don't know. He hung up pretty fast."

"Hope he doesn't keep bothering you."

"I can handle him."

"I'll talk to him if you want."

"I said I can handle it...daddy."

Mitch felt the bullseye on his ego take a direct hit. Time to drop the subject. He knew Hallie liked an occasional beer, so he stopped at a concession and ordered two. He gave one to Hallie and they headed into the flock of spectators. Hallie took his hand and weaved through the masses. Mitch was always impressed with the way beautiful women could part a crowd, so he didn't mind being led. They were almost within sight of the coleslaw pit when they could go no further. A huge man was in front of them. His leather jacket would have fit a compact car. A long ponytail hung down his back.

Hallie was determined to watch the spectacle unfolding in the pit. She tapped the big man on the shoulder. His head bent down and Hallie whispered something to him. The man straightened, put both of his massive arms forward and parted the front two rows of tourists. "There you go, little lady." The tourists just stared, not daring to complain.

Hallie thanked him and apologized to the tourists. "Daily News Reporter," she explained. She motioned Mitch to join her next to the pit. But before he could move the match started and the crowd tightened up even more.

Two average-looking young women faced each other from opposite sides of the pit. One was wearing a thong bikini. The other wore gym shorts and a tube top. They started to circle, arms extended in exaggerated wrestling positions. The crowd began to holler at the top of their lungs.

The wrestlers dove at each other and rolled in the coleslaw. Each was trying to push the other under the surface of the mushy pool. The smaller of the two was more agile. She got her opponent face down in the slaw.

At the crowd's insistence, she grabbed the strings of the woman's bathing suit top and yanked. It came free, and she waved it above her head. The crowd went wild. Suddenly she was pushed off and the larger woman leaped on her, trying to rip off her meager clothing.

Meanwhile, Mitch was having no fun at all. He was sandwiched between a big woman who smelled bad and a rude teenager who kept leaping up, trying to get a glimpse of the action.

He'd just decided to ease his way out of the crowd when the teenager fell against him. Unable to move his feet, Mitch lost his balance and toppled toward the human mountain in front of him. His beer spilled across the man's jacket.

Hallie noticed a shadow passing over her head. She caught a glimpse of Mitch Clanton sailing through the air, arms flailing. He landed in the middle of the pit, next to the two wrestlers. The crowd roared in approval. Mitch, disgusted, tried to get to his feet. But he couldn't get traction on the slippery plastic that lined the pit.

Hallie reached out and tried to help him. But before he could take her hand, one of the wrestlers pulled him down. She sat on his chest, trying to shove his head under. Tattooed from one bare breast to the other was a spider's web. In the center was the likeness of a black-widow. The sight of it had a strange effect on Mitch. He stared at the tattoo. He had a weird feeling that it was telling him something.

Mitch finally threw her off and got to the edge of the pit. Hallie helped him out. She burst out laughing at the sight of him. "Didn't I tell you this would be good for you?"

"So, you think this is funny, huh?" Mitch
got her in a bear hug. The goo drooled all over her.
To his astonishment, Hallie wrapped her hands
behind his neck, yanked him toward her and kissed
him full on the mouth. "Let's get out of here," she
said.

After escaping the crowd, they found a hose
and rinsed off the worst of the mess. Mitch wrung
out Hallie's vest and stored it in a saddlebag on his
bike.

"I know a place where we can get the rest
of this stuff off," he said.

Eight miles west of Samsula, Mitch headed
down a series of dirt roads toward a small tributary
of the St. Johns River. He stopped and unlocked a
gate into a heavily wooded property. A longtime
friend's family had owned this land for four
generations. It had one of the few untouched
springs left in Florida. Not many knew of its
existence.

Mitch parked at the end of the road. "I
think you'll like this place," he said. They walked
down an overgrown path for several hundred yards.
There was a small clearing at the boil that marked
the spring.

Hallie looked out across the crystal clear
water. "This is beautiful."

Mitch nodded. "I come here when I need to

work on tough problems...you know, with no distractions."

Hallie sat down, kicked off her shoes and stuck her toes in the water. "Am I a distraction?"

Mitch sat down next to her. "I think you can distract me all you like".

"Good...care for a swim?"

"You bet."

Before she could move, Mitch slid his hands under her and lifted Hallie up off the ground. He waded out into the spring. As they went deeper, she clung to him, trying to postpone the cold rush of the seventy two degree water. When he was chest deep he stopped, looking intently into her eyes.

"Are you sure...?" he started.

Hallie motioned him silent by putting her finger to his lips. She nodded.

Mitch took her finger into his mouth and chewed gently on it. She smiled, then reached down and unbuttoned his shirt, running her fingernails down his chest. Mitch noticed that they were both shivering. He pulled her against him tightly, enjoying the warmth that was created between them. Their lips met slowly, incrementally searching out sensations. They still trembled, but not from the cold water. Mitch was certain that the spring had never felt this good...

It was late afternoon by the time they reluctantly decided to leave. Their physical intimacy had wiped Mitch's mind clean of a lot of built up clutter. As they walked back to the motorcycle, Mitch looked up at the trees silhouetted against the dusky lavender and orange skies. Mosquito eating bats zig-zagged after invisible bugs. Large golden silk spiders stood out between the higher tree limbs. The sight made him stop in his tracks.

"What's wrong?" Hallie asked.

"Oh...I just realized... there are some loose ends I need to deal with...you know, business stuff."

"I see." Hallie sounded skeptical.

Mitch sensed that he had a major problem on his hands.

He dropped Hallie off at her place and tried to excuse himself. She was a little put off.

"So its wham, bam, thank you ma'am?" she said, only partly kidding.

"Hallie, today was the best day I've had in as long as I can remember. But something's come up."

"Business stuff?"

Mitch did not want to bring up the murder after such a memorable day.

"Please understand. I've got a lot on my mind right now."

"No room for me?"

"I've got to get some information as soon as I can."

"This is about Mark, isn't it?"

Mitch knew he was awful at lying. After some hesitation, he answered. "Yes."

Looking down, Hallie rubbed her forehead and let out an unconscious moan. "Today was the first day I felt free of all that...and now it comes back..."

"I want it to end, too, Hallie. What I'm after could help do that."

"Good night, then."

"Good night, Hallie."

Mitch cursed the night as he motored away. He hated having anything stand between himself and Hallie. But he knew things would not be right until he got to the bottom of this.

As soon as he arrived home, Mitch called the Jemisons. He got Mark's father. After restating his condolences, Mitch got to the point.

"Where's Mark's riding gear?" he asked. "Did the police take it?"

"No, the ambulance service gave it back, why do you ask?"

"Just a hunch I have to check out."

"The stuff's in the garage. I was going to give it away. You can have it if you like."

"I'd just like to look at it."

"Whatever you want."

It took the better part of Wednesday morning for Mitch Clanton to drive to Sarasota. The Jemison's were very cooperative when he got to their house. They had heard Mark talk about Mitch. They knew that their loss was shared by this stranger. Mr. Jemison showed him to the garage.

"I'll wait out here," he said. "Seeing Mark's stuff just...well, it's kind of hard..."

"I understand."

Mitch turned on the lights. Mark's motorcycle was in one corner of the garage. The riding gear was hung on the handlebars and draped over the seat. Mitch approached the machine from the front and inspected it carefully. He picked up the chest protector and helmet and examined them as well. "Damn," he muttered. "Just what I thought...he had to be the first one through the woods."

He said his goodbyes and headed back toward Daytona. As soon as he hit the highway, he got on his car phone.

"Traction Bikes," the voice on the other end said.

"May I speak to Rusty McInster, please."

"Sure, I'll get him...hang on a minute."

After a short pause, Rusty picked up the phone. "This is Rusty...can I help you?"

"This is Mitch Clanton."

"Hey Mitch."

"Listen Rusty, I need to ask you about the pre-ride at the Sand Pine Enduro.

"What about it...I already told the cops everything I know."

"I want you to level with me Rusty...did you actually ride the first leg?"

"Sure...but I didn't see nothing."

"What were the riding conditions like, Rusty?"

"What do you mean?"

"I mean, was it a fun section to ride that morning?"

"It was real tough, like always, but it was fun...I guess."

Mitch sensed that Rusty was getting nervous. "Nothing bothered you about the ride?"

"No, it was Okay."

"Did you run through many spider webs?"

"I, umm...don't remember, Mitch."

"You don't remember?"

"No. Uhh...listen, I've got to go...there's a customer...wants his bike, and..." The line went dead.

Mitch redialed the number. He learned that Rusty had just left without explanation.

CHAPTER VII

Mel Coburn was furious. He had just finished reading the draft report from Hallie Shugart. It was not what he had expected. He threw down the report in front of the other committee members. His balding head was crimson.

"What the hell is all this gibberish?" he said, pointing at the offending document.

"It's...It's so...scientific," volunteered the public relations liaison.

"Scientific! It doesn't say any damn thing at all! We were supposed to get something we could use to keep those blasted bikes off our land, not a dictionary of Latin words."

"I think those are the names of plants or animals...or something."

"I know what they are! What I don't know is what good this does us."

"The report says its a draft of her preliminary findings. Maybe she's saving the good stuff for later."

"Yeah, and maybe she's gone soft in the

head!"

"What can we do about it?"

"I know what I'm going to do. I'm going down there and have a talk with her. You know, get her back on point."

"She's not a dog, Mel."

"Lucky for her...I might have her put down."

Mel Coburn had been looking for an excuse to get out of Tallahassee for a while. He thought a trip to Daytona would be just the ticket. He was tired of kissing the asses of politicians. Besides, Mel had a new horse to try out.

That evening he gathered up his tack and got ready for an early start on Wednesday. He rose before dawn, loaded up his new sorrel quarter horse and headed down Highway 27. He was still worked up over Hallie's report, but confident that he could turn her around.

He hooked up with the interstate just north of Gainesville. At the first truck stop, he pulled off for breakfast. Sliding into a booth, he ordered his meal. A local newspaper was on the seat next to him. On the back page was an article about a new strain of oranges being developed by the University of Florida. They were supposed to be very cold tolerant. Mel loved orange juice, so he read the article with passing interest.

After breakfast, he headed out to his truck.

A young man and woman had pulled up in a green pickup truck. The entire tailgate was plastered with stickers. The man was bent over in front of Mel's truck.

"What the hell are you doing?" Mel asked.

In a strident voice, the woman spoke up. "How can you murder your brethren?"

"What are you talking about?"

"You know what I'm talking about...that!" She pointed at the rear window of his truck cab. A rifle rested there on a gun rack.

"I take it you have a problem with hunting."

"Yes. It's immoral."

"What's that you put on my bumper?"

"A warning!"

Mel walked to the front of his truck. A crooked bumper sticker had been placed over his state hunting pass. It read: SHOOT HUNTERS, NOT ANIMALS. In the corner was a small logo with the letters: CHE.

Mel was getting steamed. "What are you, a bunch of goddamn misplaced revolutionaries?"

"It stands for Citizens for Hunter Eradication."

"Swell...get away from my rig."

"Don't you know it's cruel to kill animals? How would you like it?"

"If I was a deer, maybe I could tell you."

"That's just the point, you don't know how

76

animals suffer at the hands of man."

"Are the members of your group all vegetarians?"

"Of course not."

"Well, I don't suppose livestock cares much for being killed either."

"It's not the same."

"It's never the same when the finger's pointed at you."

Mel was losing his patience. "You're lucky I don't call the police." He pushed by the woman and got in his truck.

The young man finally spoke. "It is our duty to request that you turn over your gun."

Mel acted intrigued. "To you?"

"Yes, we will see that it is destroyed."

"Well then...that's just what I'll do..."

"Do you mean that?"

"Of course I do. I'll turn it over...when pigs fly!"

The woman suddenly flew off the handle. "You just wait and see! We're ready to strike back at all you..."

Mel Coburn started his truck and pulled away, leaving her talking to thin air. She kicked at his horse trailer as it swung by. Mel shouted back at them, "Have a nice day...idiots!"

As he drove off, Mel felt an uneasiness to his anger. "And these are the nuts that think we're saving Mother Nature just for them." he lamented aloud. Relaxing his grip on the wheel a bit, he brought his attention back to the highway.

Turning east off the interstate at Ocala, he headed through the heart of Florida. After a while it occurred to him that he was near a large piece of property that the state was about to buy. Forty thousand acres of pine forest, sand scrub and wetlands would be added to the public domain. It would fill an important gap in the conservation area stretching from the Oklawaha River to Lake George. Mel had helped put the purchase together through his contacts at the Game Commission. They were almost ready to close the deal.

He pulled off the main highway to get a firsthand look at the property. It was about as unspoiled a place as Mel had ever seen. A large "For Sale" sign still stood at the edge of the road. He parked next to it, got out and peeled off the unsolicited bumper sticker. He looked longingly at a trail leading off into the woods. "Time for that another day," he told himself as he rubbed his hands together to remove bits of the sticker glue.

The rest of the trip to Daytona was uneventful. But to his surprise, he couldn't find a motel room anywhere near the city. He knew nothing about Bike Week, except that the noise from the passing motorcycles was making his horse nervous. He finally settled in at a rural mom and pop motel far from town. The accommodations were not great, but he could ride his horse into the woods right near the motel. He dug out Hallie Shugart's phone number from his wallet and gave her a call.

Hallie was preparing to leave for her study site when the phone rang. She hurried back into the apartment and answered it just as Mel was about to give up.

"Hello."

"Is this Hallie Shugart?"

"Yes."

"This is Mel Coburn."

"Oh, Mr. Coburn, how are you?"

"To tell the truth, I've been better. I need to talk to you about your study."

"Did you get the draft I sent?"

"Yeah, I got it all right."

"Is something wrong?"

"Well, you might say that. I think we need to re-examine the reasons for this study."

"Sure, go ahead."

"No, not on the phone. I'm some damn place outside Daytona. We need to meet and discuss this."

"I see...I was about to head out to one of my study areas. Maybe you'd like to come along?"

"That might be good. I'd like to see what you're doing down here."

Hallie didn't particularly like the tone of his voice.

She arranged to meet him at his motel. It was only two miles from the property where The Alligator was to be run. She had planned on taking White Fang. Mark's parents had gladly let her keep him. The dog had become a good security blanket for her. But since she wouldn't be alone today, she decided to leave him at the apartment.

When she arrived at the motel, Hallie was surprised to see Mel Coburn standing next to a horse.

"What a beautiful animal!" she said.

"Just got him."

"I thought so...he smells new," she quipped.

"Yeah, right...so where is this land you're studying?"

"It's not far from here...just down the road actually."

"Good!" he said, stroking the horse's forelock. "Maybe I'll just follow along behind you then...sort of break him in."

"Umm, I guess I could drive slow."

"Don't worry about that," he said. "This horse was built for speed."

"Anything you say."

Hallie was reluctant to complain about being held to a horse's pace. The chairman had control of the study, and she knew it. But she was already off to a late start and had planned on working until dusk. The Alligator was to be run the following day, on Thursday. It was the only enduro in Florida that was not held on a Sunday. She was worried that she wouldn't have enough data to draw conclusions from later.

It took almost an hour to reach the first study site. The chairman tied his horse to a nearby tree.

"Okay, let's see what you do at these things."

Hallie explained the sampling techniques to him and started to lay out a new transect. Mel shook his head in disapproval.

"Why are you bothering with all this? Can't you just take pictures of the damages after a race? This area looks like all the other land around here. What's the point?"

"Well, we're actually standing on last year's enduro course."

"You're pulling my leg."

"No sir...and that's the point of this study, to see if there really is any lasting damage. These trails heal over very quickly in this climate and these soil conditions. Only careful observation will determine exactly what changes occur."

"You haven't found any damage yet?"

"All the data I've collected so far is short term. I won't know what the lasting effects will be until a good year or two has passed."

"You didn't answer my question. Have you found any damage?

"Of course there are some immediate disturbances to the soil and vegetation. I described that in the draft report."

"Did you take pictures."

"Yes, I photodocument everything," she said, holding up her Polaroid camera.

"Very good. Then here's what I want you to do. After the race tomorrow, get some pictures of the torn up ground. It doesn't matter where you do it, just get good pictures. Put them together with the pre-race photos and rewrite your report so that normal people can tell that this is not the kind of thing we want on public lands! Is that clear enough?"

Hallie was crestfallen. Her hunch about the TAC group had been right. They didn't want a study, they wanted a lynching. She stared at the chairman for a long moment.

"No sir," she said.

"What did you say?"

"I said, no sir, I won't do it."

"You know I can replace you like that," he said, snapping his fingers.

"Yes sir."

"Then do yourself a favor. I'm going for a little ride down this trail. You think about what I said. When I get back, let me know what you've decided."

He left Hallie Shugart standing there and returned to his horse. He mounted up and started down the trail that she had chosen to study. The disturbance of the animals hooves made the transect useless to her.

For no particular reason, Hallie snapped a photo of the chairman as he rode by. Over his shoulder he said: "Look at the bright side. If we can get them off our land, maybe they won't end up like that racer I read about. What a way to go! ...Twenty minutes, Hallie." He rode off.

Hallie felt a dull sorrow swelling up inside her at his reference to Mark's fate. She tensed up, pushing the emotions down. There would be no more tears. She refocused on her immediate problem. So this is how it ends, she thought. She absently took the photo from the end of the automatic camera and watched it develop. In the picture, the chairman looked smug but goofy on the horse. His comb-over stood straight up on one side of his head. She noticed that his jowls flapped when he rode. Hallie Shugart walked to her truck and threw the camera and photograph on the seat. Her first impulse was to get in and drive off. But she wanted to be able to speak her mind, even though she doubted it would do any good. She sat on the tailgate and waited. Forty-five minutes went by.

She was getting mad. It was bad enough that he was forcing her off this assignment. Now he was adding insult to injury.

She knew that the trail he had taken crossed the main logging road about three miles north of her position. She decided to drive to the intersection to see if he got that far. When she arrived at the crossroads, she found no hoofprints. Maybe he had gotten lost, she reasoned. The woods were full of small side trails that led in every direction. He could have gotten turned around. She decided to go looking for him.

She slipped her truck into four-wheel drive as she turned off the logging road onto a poorly defined jeep trail. After crossing through several miles of palmetto prairie and flatwoods, she entered a dense forest. If someone was going to get lost, this was the place to do it.

The driving became more and more difficult as she went deeper into the woods. The overhanging branches seemed to press down on her. She also hated scratching up her truck this way. Hallie kept glancing at her compass to keep track of her progress. A large mud hole appeared ahead of her. There was no way around it and she didn't want to chance not making it through. There was no choice but to go back.

Putting the truck in reverse, she headed for a small clearing behind her, off to one side of the trail. As she swung the rear end around, the truck suddenly bounced and lurched to a stop. She hadn't seen the log at the edge of the clearing. It had lodged under the truck, just in front of the differential. She tried to drive off it, but it was no use. She hit the steering wheel with both fists. "Shit!" was all she could think to say.

After several attempts at using the jack to get free, she gave up. The ground was so soft that her efforts only made matters worse. She checked her cell phone. The battery was dead. She would have to walk out.

Hallie slung the compass around her neck and shoved her keys in her pants pocket. Then she grabbed her machete and canteen and started hiking back. Now she wished she had brought White Fang. Realizing that she could cut a couple of miles off her walk, she decided to head out at an angle to the trail. Hallie had never been on this part of the property before, but she was confident she could make it. The terrain was difficult, but at least it was mostly dry. The machete helped to get through the worst of the palmettos.

She followed a series of small clearings where the vegetation was not so dense. After a while, she started to feel at home again in the forest. One stuck vehicle and a ruined research project aside, it was a good day for hiking. Now and then she would pause to look at some strange insect, a darting bird or patches of colored lichens on tree bark. A small trail opened to her left, leading her through a wall of chest high gallberries. Up ahead, she saw something that looked out of place in this wilderness. It was shiny black and fluttered slightly in the breeze. Approaching cautiously, she finally made out what it was. Someone had made a makeshift tent out of plastic sheeting. It was held up by a line stretched between the trees. Cut palmetto fronds were fastened along its length for concealment. Hallie could see that someone had been there recently. A small fire still emitted a thin stream of smoke from within a circle of rocks. She had heard that there were vagrants living on the vacant land outside almost every city in Florida. But this was the first time she had actually seen one of their camps.

Nature she could deal with. Humans could be another matter entirely. She backed off and changed direction, angling away from the tent through the thicker brush. As she retreated, a hunched over figure in tattered army camo gear raised his bearded face from the nearby bushes. Leaves and twigs were entwined in his long matted brown hair, adding to his cryptic appearance. Bloodshot eyes followed her until she was out of sight. Weathered hands slowly raised a half burned joint to his lips. It glowed hot as he took a deep drag and remained motionless.

Now Hallie could no longer see where her feet landed as she walked. So she purposely trod heavily to warn off any lazy rattlers that might be in her path. Occasionally some harmless blacksnake or towhee would flush and startle her. Finally the undergrowth thinned and she relaxed again, walking with almost no sound on the damp forest floor. As she made her way into a clearing, she looked up and instantly froze. In the shade of the palmettos, the entire perimeter of the clearing was lined with large black bodies.

One of the creatures suddenly jumped to its feet. It let out a squealing snort of alarm. To Hallie's horror the entire herd of wild pigs awoke. She picked a gap between the animals and ran for it. The hogs and sows bolted in every direction. Hallie crashed through the palmettos as fast as her legs could pump. She desperately searched for a tree to climb. A huge razorback boar had chosen the same path as Hallie. It was closing on her quickly. Hallie darted to her right, hoping to get out of its way. The boar made an even tighter turn and kept coming. Hallie realized that the three hundred pound beast was after her! She headed straight for a large oak tree as the boar lowered its tusks and charged at her legs. She made a desperate leap for a low limb. Grabbing it, she pulled up with all the strength she had. One sharp tusk of the boar struck her heel as she swung her legs up around the branch. Her hiking boot absorbed the blow.

The boar circled beneath her. Its beady eyes stared up at her with unnerving intent. The limb she was on was festooned with ferns and lichens. She had to lock her hands together to keep from losing her grip. All she could do was hang helplessly under the branch, her hair less than two feet from the razorback's snout. The animal began to paw the ground, like a bull getting ready to charge. After a few grinding jaw movements to sharpen its long tusks, the hog crouched back on its hind legs, preparing to spring. Hallie squeezed her body against the tree as hard as she could. The boar leaped. Hallie screamed. A loud explosion ripped across the palmettos. The hog's snout suddenly lurched backward, saliva flying. It missed Hallie by inches and landed on its side. The second shotgun blast hit the underside of the razorback's rib cage. One size 00 buckshot penetrated its heart.

Hallie strained to look over her shoulder at the animal. It gave a two final kicks, then lay still. She waited a few moments before swinging down from the tree. Someone was walking through the palmettos toward her. She heard a pump-action shotgun being cocked.

The leaves parted and a stranger walked over to the hog. He poked the business end of the shotgun into the animals ear and pulled the trigger again, scrambling brains inside the thick skull and across the dry leaf litter. Hallie turned away from the noise and the mess. "Cain't be too careful with these critters." he said matter-of-factly.

Hallie stared at the man. He looked familiar...the short-cropped reddish hair, slightly sunburnt complexion and thin lips. But she couldn't place him.

"Thanks for shooting that...that monster!"

"He's a big-un alright. Too bad boar hogs his size don't eat so good."

Hallie went to pick up the machete that she had dropped under the oak. The stranger put his foot on it before she could pick it up.

"You won't be needin' that," he said, cocking the gun again. "I got plans fer you, little gal."

CHAPTER VIII

On the way back from Sarasota, Mitch Clanton wished he hadn't offered to represent Rusty. He didn't like the idea of defending a possible murderer. Especially this one. But what was done was done. He had let his ego get the best of him at the interrogation, and now he would just have to live with the consequences. He would try to find Rusty and talk him into coming in. But he had no idea where to start looking.

When he got back to Daytona, Mitch went to the cycle shop. The owner hadn't seen Rusty since Mitch called. One of the other mechanics told him where Rusty lived. Mitch figured it was a long shot, but he drove out to take a look around.

He was hunting for a trailer on a small woodlot. He almost drove right by it. The property was a camouflaged fortress. The barb wire fence around it had all shapes and sizes of boards, old highway signs, roofing tin and other junk weaved into it. There was even a battered surfboard. Everything had been painted brown and green to blend into the trees and shrubs.

In the middle of the property was a rundown trailer on cement blocks. There were no vehicles around, unless he counted the old gutted school bus that lay rusting on its frame. Mitch parked outside the fence and pulled open the crudely constructed gate.

He went to the trailer and knocked. A Carolina wren flew out from its nest behind the light fixture near the door, startling Mitch. There was only silence from within. He peered through the window. Against the far wall was a confederate flag. A tattered sofa took up most of the living room. Mitch cupped his hands against his temples to block out the glare. There was a table next to the window. It was covered with dishes, motorcycle parts and assorted junk. Amid the clutter were a pile of photos. He strained to get a better look. They were pictures of Hallie Shugart. It was obvious from their perspective that she had not been aware of the photographer. Mitch felt his blood start to boil. He suddenly regretted letting her out of his sight. The sooner he found her, the better he would feel. He knew she had planned on working that day, but she should be home by now.

As he headed back to his van, Mitch noticed something that he had not seen before. Near a cluster of trees was a rectangular object that rose from the ground at an angle. He walked over to it and brushed off some of the leaves. A heavy-gauge steel door was set in a raised concrete foundation. A huge padlock was fastened to the latch. Like the fence, the entire structure was painted to avoid detection. Mitch wondered if it was an old bomb shelter. A lot of them had been built in Florida during the early sixties. Mitch's parents had told him about the Cuban missile crisis. He had been too young to really understand it at the time. On instinct, he banged on the door and hollered "Anyone there?" He put his ear to the steel plate but heard nothing.

Behind the concrete bunker was a rusting fifty-five gallon drum, obviously used as a burn barrel. Mitch peered inside. Amid the torched garbage and unidentifiable melted trash were several partially burned newspapers. At first glance they looked like checkout stand tabloids. Mitch reached in an lifted out the remains of one of them. The name at the top was unfamiliar to him: The Patriot Review. He delicately spread the blackened pages. There were retrospect stories about the ATF actions at Waco, Texas and references to Ruby Ridge. From the tone of the articles, it was apparent that this was an anti-government newspaper. Advertisements for firearms, knives and mercenaries filled out the bulk of the periodical.

Mitch Clanton went back to his van and called Hallie's apartment. There was no answer.

"Don't panic," he reassured himself. "At least she's got her dog for protection."

He pressed harder on the gas pedal as he headed for Daytona. Once in town, the heavy bike traffic slowed him down to a crawl. It would soon be dark.

Hallie's truck wasn't at her apartment. To Mitch's dismay, White Fang was inside. He fished her spare key from under a flower pot and let the dog out. Judging from how long he pissed, Mitch knew Hallie hadn't been home for some time. Now he was seriously worried.

He looked at his watch. The Sand Slingers meeting should be starting about now. Mitch hoped that one of them would know where she was. He put White Fang in his van and headed across town to the old city administration building where the bike club met.

When he got there, Mitch searched the long deserted corridors for the meeting room. He finally located it on the second floor. When he walked in, there was a lively discussion in progress. The club president was holding up a letter. It was from the Citizens for Hunter Eradication. No one there had ever heard of the group. The letter threatened violence if they did not call off the Alligator Enduro.

"These dummy's think were holding some kind of alligator roundup!" Sam Braselton was saying in disbelief.

Joe Brown, a wiry and experienced rider, was in charge of the course layout. He spoke up. "Just what we needed. It's not bad enough we had a rider killed, now we've got to worry about these nuts!"

"What's the status of getting help from the other clubs for security?" Wayne Lenoir asked.

"Doesn't look good," said Joe. "We've got enough to man the checkpoints. But there wasn't time to get extras, especially for a weekday race. We're going to have to do our own continuous security sweeps."

"What if the pre-riders stay on their sections throughout the race?" Sam suggested.

"That's about all we can do at this point," Joe agreed.

Mitch walked to the front table and put his hands up to get their attention. They fell silent.

"Does anyone here know where Hallie Shugart is."

"What for, you old letcher," someone in the back said.

"I think she may be in trouble. She was going out to work on The Alligator today, but she's not back yet."

"I never thought a young lady like that should be running around in the woods by herself," Paul Wedgefield said.

"Does anyone want to come and help me look for her?"

Joe Brown gave Mitch a doubtful look. "That would be like finding a needle in a haystack," he said. "There's over twenty thousand acres of land out there. It's hard enough to find someone in the daytime. Are you sure that's where she is?"

"No, but it's the only place I know to look."

"We'll try to help you then...but like I say, I wouldn't get my hopes up."

"Thanks...oh, I almost forgot...does anyone know where Rusty McInster is?"

"I talked to him this afternoon. He's supposed to be helping with the race tomorrow," Sam said.

"Good, I need to see him."

Sam, Paul, Wayne and Joe left with Mitch. He got White Fang out of his van to take with them. They piled into Joe and Sam's four-wheelers, stopping at Paul's place to get more flashlights before heading out of town. When they got to the property, they split up to search in different directions. Mitch decided to go with Wayne and Joe. They would head northeast.

"Wayne," Joe said. "You should drive."

"How come?" asked Mitch.

"Wayne's half Cherokee, he can track a snow flake in a blizzard."

It was a pitch black night. They drove the main logging roads, looking for fresh tire tracks. It hadn't rained for almost a week, so the tire marks were hard to see on the dry sand. Wayne spotted a set that he thought were the most recent. They followed them for several miles. Then he began to slow down. "We lost 'em," Wayne said.

"Maybe she turned off the main road," Joe offered. "There's a few cross trails back the way we came, but they're pretty rough."

Wayne turned around and retraced their route. He found where Hallie had turned toward the woods. They followed the trail until they came to her disabled truck. Mitch jumped out and looked it over.

"She's not here."

He hollered out her name and listened for a reply. None came.

Mitch shined a flashlight into her truck. He opened the door and found the photograph she had taken that day. He recognized Mel Coburn. The others had gathered next to the truck with him.

"Look at this photo," Mitch said. "This guy on the horse is the state trails chairman from Tallahassee. What the hell is he doing here?"

Joe Brown took the photo and studied it. "See the pink ribbon on that tree. This has to be on the last section of the enduro. We ran out of orange. Can't tell what part of the loop it is, though."

They hooked Wayne's truck up to Hallie's and pulled it off the log. If she came back to it, she could drive out. Mitch got White Fang out of the back of Joe's vehicle. He had no idea if this would work. Pointing to the ground near the truck, he encouraged the dog. "Go find her!"

The dog looked around excitedly. Mitch pointed to the ground again.

"Sniff her out, boy...here!"

White Fang circled a few times, then started off into the woods. Mitch wished he had thought to bring a leash. He tightened his grip on the flashlight and set out after the shepherd.

"You guys stay here!" he yelled back.

He could hear White Fang moving through the underbrush. Mitch struggled to keep up, scratching his shins on the sawtoothed palmetto stems. Suddenly, he heard wild barking in the distance. Gaining hope, he hurried toward the sound. He found White Fang jumping up against the base of a large tree. Mitch swung the flashlight up through the limbs. Two yellow eyes glowed back at him. A bobcat leaped to the ground and shot off through the underbrush. Mitch grabbed White Fang's collar as the dog sprang to give chase. Man and dog hit the ground and rolled to a stop. "Good try, boy," he said, trying to calm the excited shepherd. He picked up the dog and walked back toward the distant headlights.

"Any luck?" Joe asked as Mitch approached.

"No...It was a long shot anyway. Wayne, can you track someone in this terrain?"

"I know enough about tracking not to try it at night...we'd all get lost out here."

They yelled Hallie's name a few more times into the darkness before giving up. On the way out they stopped every half mile or so to shout and blow the horn. They heard nothing in return.

It was past 2:00 a.m. before they got back to the highway and met up with the others.

"Do you think we should call the cops?" Paul asked.

"I'll talk to them," Mitch said. "But I don't think they're going to do anything tonight. They have their hands full with all the bikers in town."

When they dropped him off at his van, Mitch thanked them for their help. He agreed to pre-ride and take security on the last loop the next morning. They gave him a map of the course and directions to the beginning of his section. He would ride it first thing in the morning to see if he could find any trace of Hallie.

Mitch Clanton went home and tried to sleep. But lying there in bed only made him feel helpless. His call to the sheriff's office had been an exercise in futility. He had to admit that there had been no signs of foul play. They told him that a deputy might be sent out the next morning. Apparently Hallie had not been gone long enough to qualify as a missing person. Mitch got up and went to his dining room to look at the map again. He pulled the retractable light down close to the paper. Hallie's truck was a good half mile from the race course. Maybe the horse had gotten away from them and they were looking for it when she got stuck, he figured. He tried to imagine where Hallie and Coburn might have gone. He traced a path with his finger along the roads near the truck. About a mile away was an old rock pit. Mitch used to swim in the quarry when he was a kid. The landowner had eventually posted No Swimming signs, fearing that someone would get hurt jumping off the steep, high walls. Just thinking about the pit, Mitch could almost feel the giddy freefall in his gut from countless childhood leaps. He also thought about the small alligators they used to pelt with rocks. The gators would be grown up by now. He hoped that Hallie had not gone that way in the dark.

Mitch went to his living room. He leaned back in his easy chair and tried to clear his mind. He had to try and make sense of things. So many questions but few answers. If only he had more to go on, he thought, then he could figure this thing out. The idea of Hallie lost out in the woods at night with a murderer on the loose was almost more than he could stand. At least she was likely not alone. If Rusty showed at the race it could clear things up. He shut his eyes and began to plan out his actions for the next day. Slowly, his chin started to sag toward his chest. Waves of tiredness washed against the back of his eyes, pulling him irresistibly into a warm, comforting place...

CHAPTER IX

In the darkness, Hallie Shugart struggled with her bonds. The nylon rope was cutting into her wrists. She could feel every heartbeat throbbing in her hands. The cast iron stove she was tied to had a projection that stuck into her back.

The last eight hours had been a nightmare. The stranger had held her at gunpoint, blindfolded her and made her walk deeper into the woods. He didn't put a gag on her. He said she could scream all she liked, nobody would hear her. He had tied a leather thong around her neck and made her walk in front. He laughed at her when she tripped and fell. Then he helped her up and brushed her off, his hands lingering too long on parts of her body. He scolded her for not being more careful. Hallie had never been so scared in her life. She thought back to every abduction crime report she could remember, trying to dwell on cases that did not end up in the obituary column. There weren't many. As Hallie stumbled along, she got hold of herself and slowly fought down the fear. Through sheer will, she forced her analytical side to take over. Only a clear mind could find a way out of this, and she knew it. Suddenly they came to a structure of some kind. Although she couldn't see, Hallie knew she had been brought to an old shack. The creaking steps, sagging floorboards and smell of rotting wood gave it away.

He bound her hands and tied her to the stove. Then he took off the blindfold. She saw that it was indeed an old cabin. Judging from the litter of empty shotgun shells and beer cans, it was once used by hunters. On the floor across from her was Mel Coburn. He didn't look good. There was a gash across his forehead and he wasn't moving. He was tied up with an assortment of ropes.

Her captor left her there, saying he was going out to hunt something for them to eat. When he was gone, Hallie tried to get Mel to talk.

"Mr. Coburn...are you alright?"

No reply.

Hallie scooted around the stove as far as she could toward him. She could just reach his stomach with her left foot. She poked him.

"Mr. Coburn."

She poked again.

"Uhhhnn..." he groaned.

Hallie breathed a sigh of relief.

After some time had passed, Mel was able to speak. Hallie learned that he had been stopped by the stranger on a nearby trail. Said he was trespassing. Mel had to dismount when he was threatened with a shotgun. While he was trying to reason with him, the man got mad. He hit Mel across the head with the barrel of the gun. Mel vaguely remembered being brought to the old camp in the back of a truck. After that he was trussed up.

"How did you get here?"

"My truck got stuck while I was out looking for you," Hallie said with a hint of disdain. "He shot a big razorback that was after me, then he forced me to come here."

"Sorry I got us into this mess. I got turned around in these woods. Guess I stumbled into the wrong guy."

"Guess we both did."

For the next couple of hours they talked on and off about their situation. They knew they weren't on the enduro course, so it wasn't likely that anyone in the race would find them. They both worked on untying themselves, but it was hopeless.

Finally, they heard footsteps outside, then the sound of someone chopping wood. Some time later they smelled smoke. Their captor entered the shack, went straight to Hallie and pulled out his hunting knife. She fixed her eyes on his. If he was going to kill her, she wasn't going to make it easy. He bent down and with a quick swipe of the blade, cut her hands free.

"Don't be stupid, now" he said. "This knife's sharp enough to shave a rat and not wake him. You try'n run and I'll gut that flabby sumbitch next to you."

He took her outside. Hallie looked around for any clue that would tell her where she was. An old pickup truck was parked next to Mel's horse. The horse was tied to a tree. In every direction, the woods looked the same.

The man told her she was going to help cook their dinner. The cook fire was settling down to a low flame. Some water was on to boil.

He reached into a sack and pulled out a large dead rattlesnake. Its head was connected to the body only by a scrap of skin. The man handed her the front end and told her to hold it tight so he could skin it.

She took the snake's head. Hallie watched as he skillfully split the hide down the length of the body.

"Ever eat snake?" he asked.

"No."

"Real good meat...better'n possum."

"That's comforting."

After he skinned and gutted the carcass, he started to hand it to her. "Forgot my manners," he said, offering his slimy hand to her. "Never interduced myself...name's Thad...Thad Henry."

Hallie felt like she was being tested. She

reached out and shook his hand. He passed her the snake and she laid it on a wire grill over the fire. Thad cut up a white, starchy-looking plant material that Hallie didn't recognize. He put it in the boiling water.

Their dinner had been unusual. She had never eaten rattlesnake nor heart of cabbage palm before. She hated to admit it, but it wasn't half as bad as she thought it would be. When they had finished eating, he told Hallie to feed the leftovers to Mel. She went inside, kneeled next to him and propped his head up on her thigh. His wound had scabbed over. It needed some stitches, but it wasn't too serious. Hallie tore the snake meat into small pieces and fed it to him. She didn't tell him what it was. When she was done, she went back outside, but not before hiding her truck keys and tossing the rattler's head in the stove. Thad was sitting on the bottom step.

"What do you want with us?"

"You was the only one I wanted."

"What about Mr. Coburn?"

"That cuss? I didn't s'pect you to have nobody with you today. I need to think some on what to do with him."

"So you followed me here?"

"Yer easy to follow," he grinned.

"What are you going to do with us?"

"That's up to you."

"What do you mean?"

"I mean a pretty thing like you needs a man what can take care o' her." He watched for a reaction. When he got none, he continued. "Things is changin' fast these days. It'll be up to the common man to take care of theyselves real soon, and I aim to be ready."

"What if I don't want a man to take care of me?"

He squinted at her for some time.

"Some folks don't know what's best for 'em. Sometimes a man's just got to take things into his own hands, knowin' it'll work out. B'sides, you could do a lot worse."

"Hardly."

Thad slowly rose to his feet and stood in front of her. When his hand whipped around, Hallie had no time to duck. He backhanded her hard across the cheek. She went down on one knee.

"Don't sass me, girl!" he shouted. "My women don't sass their man!" He reared back to kick, but stopped to think about it. He reached out and stroked her hair gently. "There...now, don't you mind my temper."

Hallie cradled the right side of her face in her hand. It stung like fire. And her ears were ringing. Oh God...he's serious about this, she thought. She decided to change tactics.

"A girl needs time to get used to a new

man," she said, faking a sob.

"Didn't take you long to get used to that lawyer fella."

"We're just friends."

"Don't tell me lies. I know different. Anyhow, I seen you two at the wreslin' contest."

That's why he looks familiar, Hallie thought. "We were just having some fun," she said.

"Well, I'm gonna' pay him a visit. Maybe then you and I can have some a' that fun."

Hallie's mind reeled. The man was very unstable, probably psychotic. And possibly Mark's killer. Escape was her only hope. She couldn't dwell on what he might do to her. She had to create an opening. Her life, and maybe Mitch's, depended on it. The hatred she felt was like nothing she had experienced before. But he had the upper hand.

"You don't need to do that," Hallie said. "We can have all the fun you want if you just stay here."

Shaking his head, he gave her a disgusted look. "It ain't right to be with another man's woman. Not so long as he's alive, anyways. Besides, cain't have him snoopin' around no more."

"But we're not really..."

Nostrils flaring, he rushed at her and kicked her in the side. Hallie went sprawling, face down in the dirt. He kneeled on her back and leaned close to her ear.

"What did I tell you about lyin'?"

Hallie couldn't reply. He picked her up by the back of the neck, shaking her as he took her into the shack and tied her up again. Angrily, he went outside and drove away.

It was going to be a long night. Hallie wasn't religious, but she prayed silently that the man would not find Mitch. She couldn't explain how attached to Mitch she had become in so short a time. Thinking about it now, she realized that Mitch was a lot like her father. They were both compassionate and gentle, and treated her as an equal. She had lost one of them. The thought of losing the other one was unbearable.

As she tried to find a more comfortable position, Hallie noticed a small, sharp burr on the leg of the stove. She slid the rope over it and started moving it up and down, pulling forward at the same time. The tension on the rope made her wrists hurt even more, but she felt a small strand of the nylon give way.

CHAPTER X

Mitch was on his dirt bike. It was almost dark out. Through the gloom, he could barely see Hallie ahead of him. She was riding Mark Jemison's bike. It looked like she was driving into a fog. He called to her to hold up, but she just laughed and went faster. Her hair stood out in the slipstream behind her head. He didn't like that she wasn't wearing a helmet. Didn't she know it was too dangerous? Why couldn't he catch her, he wondered? The faster he tried to go, the further ahead she got. He opened his mouth wide to holler as loud as he could. At that instant he went face first into a spider's web. A huge spider was caught between its web and his face. He tried to shake it off, but with no luck. It turned and crawled straight into his mouth...

Mitch sat bolt upright in his easy chair. He was suddenly wide awake. Heart pounding, he felt the cold sweat breaking on his brow. To his astonishment, it was light outside. He jumped up and checked his watch. It was 8:05.

Within minutes, Mitch had hooked up his cycle trailer, thrown his gear in the van and was heading toward The Alligator with a cup of coffee in his hand. As he turned onto the two-lane blacktop outside of town, he cranked the van up to seventy-five miles per hour. He wanted to get there before the race started. Ahead, he saw the blinking red light at Pioneer Trail Road.

As he applied the brakes, something felt wrong. Suddenly his foot went to the floor. His brakes were gone. To his right, a semi was heading for the intersection. He grabbed the emergency brake and pulled. Nothing happened. The semi blew its air horn in warning. Mitch could see smoke coming off its tires. They were going to meet at the intersection.

Mitch slammed the van into park. The rear wheels locked up. He was still doing forty when he ran out of time. He spun the wheel hard right to avoid the semi. The van went sideways as it dropped halfway into the roadside ditch. Dirt and sod flew as it grounded out and skidded to a jarring halt against a culvert.

Mitch jumped out of the van. He wasn't hurt, but the adrenaline in his bloodstream had put his instant coffee to shame. He could see that his van wasn't going anywhere. The trucker had pulled onto the road shoulder past the intersection. After a few moments, he got out and walked over to

Mitch.

"You alright?" he asked.

"Yeah. Sorry about what happened...my brakes went out."

"I'll say they did. I called the sheriff's department. Told them you might need a wrecker."

"Thanks."

"Sure thing, pal...good luck."

As the trucker left, Mitch assessed his situation. He knew that a traffic investigation and tow could shoot the whole morning. He decided to leave a note on the van and use his motorcycle to get to The Alligator.

He put on his riding gear and unloaded his bike. He filled it with gas and was about to start it when he heard a siren behind him. An unmarked sheriff's car pulled up to him. Charlie Dorge stepped out.

"Well, well, well...what do we have here? It wouldn't be Mitchell Clanton leaving the scene of an accident?"

Mitch considered him with utter disdain. "Charlie, I've got to get to the Alligator Enduro. Hallie's been gone all night and I think she's lost out there."

"Is that so? You and her wouldn't be up to a little hanky-panky, would you?"

"So help me Charlie, if you don't back off..."

"You'll do what?" the detective said, patting his concealed revolver.

Mitch yanked off his riding gloves and threw them onto his trailer.

"I have to find her!"

"Now don't get your panties in a bunch. I've got this thing under control."

"You know where Hallie is?"

"No, but I know who the killer is."

"Who is it?"

"You remember Woody Moseler, don't you? When we were kids we used to call him Mossback, after the time he glued Spanish moss all over himself and scared those boy scouts out of their pants."

"Yeah, yeah...people were reporting skunk apes for years after that...get to the point!"

"You're lucky I'm telling you anything, so shut up and learn something, Okay?"

Mitch removed his helmet. "So what about the old hermit?"

"We've been yanking his marijuana plants out of the woods around here for years. Of course, he's too smart to ever have any on him. We can rarely find him anyway. Last year he caught some kids harvesting his crop. He tied them up and rolled them in poison ivy. The kids said he threatened to send them back to their parents in small pieces if they came into his woods again. We should have known then that he was becoming dangerous."

"So how does all that relate to Mark?"

Charlie Dorge pulled out a pack of cigarettes, tapped one out and slowly lit it as he leaned against Mitch's van.

"I'm getting to that. Yesterday our chopper pilot found one of Mossback's camps not too far from the homicide. We checked it out and found that roll of wire we were looking for...it matches what was strung between the trees."

"So you think he was protecting his turf...trying to keep us away from his pot fields?"

"That's how I figure it. He's a Vietnam vet, so gorilla tactics would come naturally to him."

"You caught him yet?"

"He's not in custody, but I'm about to change that. Some cattlemen spotted him at another one of his camps northwest of here. I was heading there just now."

"That would put him near where The Alligator is being run today."

"You better hope it's not."

"I need to get over there."

"No, what you need to do is stay right here and take care of this little accident of yours. You're blocking part of the road."

A patrol car was approaching from the east, lights flashing. It pulled up behind the detective's vehicle and a deputy got out. After exchanging greetings, Dorge pointed at Mitch and gave the officer an order.

"You make sure he stays put until this accident is cleared up. I need to go pick up a perp out near the cycle races."

Dorge got in his car and peeled out on the highway blacktop. Mitch watched him disappear into the distance. He got off his bike and sat on the trailer, cradling his head in his hands.

"Did anyone call for a wrecker?" the officer asked.

Mitch thought for a moment.

"No...guess I need one."

As the officer returned to his patrol car to use the radio, Mitch put his helmet on and got back on his bike. As soon as the officer sat down in the car, Mitch started the bike and took off down the road shoulder. He tried to accelerate harder, but the engine hadn't had a chance to warm up. It sputtered and missed as he adjusted the choke. It was only a few seconds before he heard the siren behind him. He had planned on going cross-country to The Alligator, but not just yet.

When the patrol car drew near, Mitch jumped the bike over the roadside ditch. The officer caught up with him and got on his bullhorn. He ordered Mitch to stop and get off the bike. Mitch knew he had to buy some time. Up ahead was a dirt road he needed to take. But he didn't want the deputy up with him when he got there. Mitch slowed down, then stopped and shut off the bike. He was still on the far side of the ditch. The officer got out and walked around the car to confront him. As the deputy motioned him to come back across the ditch, Mitch fired up his bike. He slammed it into gear and accelerated toward the dirt road. He got there well ahead of the deputy.

As he screamed down the side road, Mitch looked back over his shoulder. The deputy was gaining on him. He crouched low on the bike and coaxed it up to seventy-three miles per hour. The patrolman was still closing the gap between them.

Mitch could see the place up ahead where he had to turn into the woods. He waited to the last second, then locked the brakes. He skidded sideways toward the opening in the trees. As he entered the woods, he heard the patrol car grinding past, trying to stop. He had made it. Mitch knew this area of the county well. He could cut about six miles off the trip by going through these woods to The Alligator. He might even beat Dorge there.

By the time he got to the race site, it was after nine o'clock. He went to the start area to see what he could find out. He found Sam Braselton.

"Has anyone seen Hallie?"

"Not that I know of. So you haven't had any luck?"

"No."

"Did you pre-ride the last loop?"

"Not yet...I got held up. I'm heading out there now. Is Rusty here"?

"He was here a little while ago. He and his cousin took the gas truck to the fuel stop."

"How about detective Dorge?"

"Haven't seen him."

"You probably will...but don't tell him I'm here."

Mitch went to the gas stop. When he got there, the two cousins were involved in an argument. They stopped when they saw Mitch approaching.

When he pulled up and shut off his bike, Rusty was the first to speak.

"Hey Mitch! You working the race today too?"

Mitch was too tired and worried to make small talk.

"Have either of you seen Hallie Shugart?"

They glanced at each other, then shrugged their shoulders.

"Rusty, I need to talk to you...in private. Let's go over here." He pointed to the cluster of trees where Rusty had parked his motorcycle. Rusty hesitated, then followed Mitch there.

Mitch started in, trying to remain calm. "I want to know what the hell is going on?"

"What do you mean, Mitch?"

"I mean, why did you lie about pre-riding the first section of the Sand Pine?"

"But...Mitch...I...just messed up. My bike wasn't running good and I was real tired that morning. After it happened, I was scared that you...you all would blame me for not riding the section. So I just said I rode it. Dang it...I...I didn't think it would matter."

"What about the pictures of Hallie?"

"What pictures?"

"You know what I'm talking about!" Mitch demanded as he grabbed two fistfuls of Rusty's jersey.

"Okay, okay, so I took some pictures of her. Is that against the law?"

"Why'd you do that?"

"I had a thing about her. I got over it."

He stared hard at Rusty. He looked repentant, but Mitch wasn't sure. Suddenly he heard himself saying, "If you're lying to me and something's happened to Hallie...the law won't have to deal with you...not after I'm through with you."

Mitch released Rusty and walked back to the gas truck. "You guys better get those gas cans unloaded and spread out. They'll be here before you know it."

He got on his bike and headed for the last loop of the race. When he had gone, Rusty and his cousin renewed their argument.

"You can't do this to me!" Rusty insisted. "Not after what we've been through...besides, the cops will bust us both!"

Without warning, Rusty's cousin struck him hard on the jaw. Rusty fell to the ground. Before he could move he was pinned. His cousin grabbed him by the hair and slammed his head against the ground. After four sharp blows, Rusty gratefully lost consciousness. The last thing he saw was his cousin's sweaty face, teeth clenched in a maniacal smile. Working quickly, he dragged Rusty by the heels and hid him in the bushes. Then he got in the truck and started down the road after Mitch Clanton. A trail of dust rose above the palmettos in the distance, marking Mitch's position.

When he was almost due east of the lone rider, he stopped the fuel truck. After testing the wind, he ran to the back of the flatbed and unscrewed the spout from the nearest gas can. As he walked along the road, he poured part of the gasoline on the palmettos. He grabbed another can an did the same with it. Again and again he poured part of each can out, moving further down the road each time. He made a continuous line of gasoline for several hundred yards. He then pulled out a cigarette lighter. As he crouched to set the fire, the lighter touched off the gas fumes. The blast of heat made him drop the lighter into the flames.

He retreated to the truck, shielding his face from a hundred gallons of gasoline going up in smoke. The flames raced along the dry ground, jumping over the shrubs like a whirlwind. The easterly breeze quickly caught and spread the fire. Within minutes it stretched for over a mile. It had been twelve years since this area had burned, and it was overripe with woody fuel. The dry palmettos and brush went up like willing tinder.

He jumped in the truck and drove back to the gas stop. When he got there, Rusty was still unconscious. He unloaded the gas cans along the side of the road, where the racers would be expecting them. Then he put on his cousin's riding gear and took off on Rusty's bike.

CHAPTER XI

Mitch Clanton wasn't sure he was in the right place. He knew he was near the last loop, but he couldn't find any of the course arrows. He was angling across a wide flatwoods when he first saw the smoke.

The gray plume was growing larger very fast. Mitch wondered if someone had gotten careless with a cigarette. But he hadn't seen any spectators around, only Rusty and his cousin. He slowed down to consider what to do.

The fire was closing in behind him. He couldn't go back the way he had come, so he kept moving. The trail he was on came to a tee at a barbwire fence. He went right and picked up speed. Looking back at the fire, he didn't see the loose coil of barbwire hanging off a fencepost. He ran it over. It caught on his rear tire, then wrapped around the sprocket hub. When it pulled tight the bike stopped. But Mitch didn't. He flew over the handlebars, banging his knees painfully on the crossbar.

Mitch picked himself up and limped back to his bike. He looked at the advancing fire. It was now close enough that he could see the flames. His actions became urgent. The wire was pulled very tightly around the hub. He needed the pair of side cutters in his fanny pack. But when he reached for it he realized that he had left it in his van. He tried to unwind the barbwire, but it wouldn't budge. He would have to break it. Grabbing the wire with both hands near the sprocket, he started bending it back and forth. He kept looking up at the fire. It was getting too close.

The wire was heating up from the friction of bending. He hadn't had time to put his gloves back on when he evaded the deputy, and the hot wire burned his fingers. He kept working it. Finally it broke. Mitch got the bike up and kicked it. But it wouldn't start. He tried again and again. Lying on its side had flooded the carburetor.

Now Mitch was concerned for his life. He knew he couldn't outrun the fire on foot. With no tools, drying off the sparkplug was out of the question. He pulled in the clutch, put it in second gear, and started to push the motorcycle. He screamed involuntarily at the effort of overcoming the clutch drag. Finally he had it moving fast enough to bump start. He threw himself on the bike and let out the clutch. It coughed once, then roared to life. Mitch shifted gears and tore down the trail.

Now he was riding in a state of sheer desperation. The wall of flames threatened to cut him off from his only escape route, which lay straight ahead. Torn between the desire for speed and the need to avoid a crash, Mitch turned up the throttle. He was running parallel to the fence. The flames were moving rapidly toward him from the right. He could already feel the heat building up. He considered trying to work the bike through the fence. Then he could ride directly away from the advancing danger. But trying to outrun a fire through the thick palmettos would be suicide.

For a moment the wind slacked and the flames stood straight up. They were now only twenty feet to the right of the trail, towering over the lone rider. Mitch was crouched on the left side of his machine, using it as a shield against the heat. Ahead, he saw a small but dense cluster of cypress trees. He recognized it as a small swamp. To his horror, he also saw that the flames were much further ahead than he had thought. Now the wind was beginning to blow again. He thought if he could reach the trees, it might be wet enough to keep the fire from burning through. It did not appear to Mitch that he could make it. But there was no other choice.

The fire now roared almost against the fenceline. The heat was becoming unbearable. He wrapped himself further around the left side of his motorcycle. His right hand felt like it was on fire. He sucked air though clenched teeth to try to cool it down. Every time he tried to wet his lips, his tongue was burned. The protective riding gear was all that stood between him and almost certain death. His lungs burned as he turned the throttle wide open and aimed for a small opening in the center of the trees.

Completely out of control, Mitch glanced off half a dozen trees before falling on his burning right side. A hiss and plume of steam came from the motorcycle as he landed in a pool of shallow water. The roar of the fire was deafening. He knew he was being surrounded.

As a kid, Mitch had seen a Disney movie about a great forest fire out West. He remembered what the firefighters had done when they were trapped. Rolling away from his bike, he began to bury himself in the black mud. Using a swimming motion, Mitch managed to work his legs and most of his body beneath the organic ooze. Leaving his helmet and goggles on, he pressed the right side of his head down. He stopped when the water just reached his nostrils. He then heaped mud over his neck and shoulders. The cool muck eased some of the pain from the burns, but it was becoming more difficult to breathe. He had to suck in much more air than normal just to keep from passing out. If the fire did not pass soon, he felt sure that he would suffocate.

Mitch shut his eyes and tried to calm himself. The fire was now almost completely around him. He lay there motionless, waiting for the fire to either kill him or spare him. The crown of a slash pine at the edge of the swamp suddenly ignited, showering him with burning embers. Several deer, panicked by the fire, raced directly over Mitch and his motorcycle. The lead buck planted a sharp hoof directly into the left side of Mitch's back, at a seam in his chest protector. One of his ribs gave way with a crack. The pain of the broken bone now competed with second degree burns for his undivided attention. Mitch rolled to his right side in an attempt to escape the pain. He curled into a fetal position. Any moment, he thought, he would black out and never wake up. It was that simple.

He stayed that way for what seemed to him an eternity. All he could do was listen to the fierce moaning and crackling of the fire. Slowly, the sound began to diminish. To his surprise, Mitch realized that he was shivering from the cool mud, which had been unaffected by the passing fire.

When he was sure the fire had gone, he sat up to take stock of his condition. "Just a flesh wound or two," he told himself, examining his broken rib with his left hand. Breathing had become a painful exercise, but he found that he could move about without too much difficulty. The back of his right hand was already starting to grow large blisters. He smeared mud on it to help stop the pain.

The motorcycle had fared better than Mitch. It had not been damaged other than a melted tank shroud, bent handguard and a broken headlight. He righted the bike and leaned it against a tree. After washing off the mud as best he could with the dark swampy water, he hung his goggles and helmet from the handlebars and walked to the edge of the wetland to see what remained of the fire.

Mitch knew that Florida's piney flatwoods thrived on fire. In fact, they depended on it to keep out the oaks that could eventually take over. He was always amazed that any forest could survive such a holocaust. The scene that surrounded him had no resemblance to the lush green woods that existed only half an hour before. The landscape now resembled some deranged painter's study in black and white. Smoldering palmetto trunks, running horizontally for most of their length, stood out in dark contrast to the light ash-covered ground. The residual heat pulsed against his face with each puff of wind. The only green remaining was well above eye level, where the taller pines had managed to keep some of their needles.

To the west, Mitch could see the fire wall moving steadily away from him. It was beginning to die out as it reached a large marsh known locally as Buttermilk Flats. He doubted that the fire could have been accidental. His worst fears about Rusty were realized, and it had almost cost him his life. A renewed sense of urgency struck him. He needed to confront Rusty again and this time get some answers. He returned to his bike, got it running and started back through the seared flatwoods.

He went to the gas stop. A number of competitors were there, taking on fuel. Rusty and his cousin were nowhere in sight. No one there had seen anyone manning the gas stop. He noticed that Rusty's bike was gone. A single set of tire tracks led northeast. Mitch decided to head that way.

CHAPTER XII

It was well after sun-up by the time Hallie Shugart had managed to saw through the ropes around her wrists. After that, she worked on the knots in Mel Coburn's bonds. Finally they were both free. At first attempt, Mel couldn't stand. The circulation in his legs had been cut off for too long. Hallie grabbed his ankles and worked his knees back and forth to restore the blood flow. As Mel's numbed limbs woke up to the pain, he gritted his teeth and gasped for air. At last he could walk. Hallie supported him outside to his horse. With her help, he managed to make it into the saddle. Hallie untied the horse and pulled herself up behind Mel.

"Are you going to be able to do this?" she asked him.

"I'm kind of dizzy, but I can ride. Which way should we go?"

"I think we should go that way," she said, pointing over his shoulder. "He took my compass, so I'm not exactly sure."

"Hold on," he said as he touched the

horse's flanks.

The trail wandered through the forest, branching off into smaller paths. They stayed on the main trail. After a few more minutes, they heard a vehicle approaching. It suddenly rounded the bend in front of them. Heading straight at them, the driver leaned on the horn. Hallie tried to hang on when the horse reared. She grabbed for Mel Coburn and got his shirt. As her weight snapped her arms straight, the cloth ripped. She went over backwards and landed hard on the ground. As Hallie struggled to regain her senses, she heard the horse galloping away with Mel. Then there was silence.

She was on her back, looking straight up at the sky between the trees. A figure abruptly bent over her, blocking the light. All she could see was a dark silhouette. The man slowly knelt beside her. When Hallie's saw his face, her heart sank.

Thad Henry reached down and squeezed her cheeks between his thumb and fingers. He rolled her head first one way, then the other.

"Yer Okay," he said.

"No thanks to you."

"What did I say 'bout sassin' me?" He drew his hand back menacingly.

"Please don't hit me again."

"That's better. Now you and me is going back to camp...we got unfinished bidness."

He pulled Hallie to her feet and made her get in the truck. Rusty's motorcycle was tied down in the back. After grinding the starter for some time, Thad got the truck started.

Hallie was fighting back tears as they returned to the shack. She hoped that Mel would bring help soon. But she knew he was still lost and it could be a while before anyone would come looking for her.

Thad parked the truck, grabbed Hallie's arm and yanked her out the driver's side. He half dragged, half carried her to the cabin. At the steps he shoved her sprawling toward the small porch. Then he took out his knife.

"I tried to be nice with you," he started. "But you won't have none of it. Maybe you like your men rough...show you who's boss...that it?"

Hallie scrambled into the shack on her hands and knees.

"Hidin' in there won't do you no good. Yer jus' making things harder."

He was about to go after her when he saw her in the doorway. Slowly, Hallie walked out of the shack, to the top of the steps. Her head was down and her hands were behind her back. She was trembling.

"That's better Sugar, it won't be so bad... you'll see. Our ways are better."

The name he called her stung her memory

like salt on a wound. She fought to control her fear and anger.

"What ways are those?" she asked.

"You don't have to be a lamb brought to slaughter by the government."

"What are you talking about?"

"You know...the fed'ral government. They want to control everything...they'll run your whole life. Even decide who lives or dies. It's aw'ready started...don't you read the papers?"

"What does the federal government have to do with me?"

"They want you to interbreed with them lower races. Soon there won't be any pure white Aryans left if we don't do somethin'. That's where we figger in."

"We?"

"A'course!" Thad explained. "I got to have a good Aryan woman to live with me and have babies! To start a new American country! Used to be a man could live in peace, by his own law...that was the real America. But they's taken that from us...now we got to start over...but this time we'll keep the coloreds blood out!" he spat the last few words out with a stream of tobacco juice.

Hallie had watched enough television documentaries to know about Adolf Hitler's use of the Aryan superiority myth. She also knew that some modern racists had adopted the dead Fuhrer's ideas. The whole concept made her skin crawl. She pondered her position as she watched the blade of Thad Henry's knife start to drop slightly.

"So you want me because I'm Aryan...but don't I have any say in this?" She asked.

"You can have a say...after you join us."

"There's more of you?"

"Sure, hundreds, maybe thousands. Right now we're kinda' scattered, but we got a place in Alabama. It's going to be the new capitol of the country. That's where I'm takin' you."

A vacant look came over Thad's eyes as he thought about his promised land. The knife in his hand was now pointed at the ground. Hallie slowly moved to her right, toward the nearby woods. Thad snapped back to reality.

"First I got to prove that I'm man enough for you. But I don't wanna' hurt ya... 'less I got to."

Hallie stopped moving.

"I don't want to get hurt."

"So why don't you jus' make this easy on yoursef'?"

"You promise not to hurt me?"

"Cross my heart."

"Could you put the knife down?"

Thad looked at the knife in his hand. Without replying, he slowly slid it back into its sheath. "Don't go reachin' for it."

"I won't"

He took off his belt and laid it on a log next to the fire pit. Hallie moved down the steps to face him. Thad moved closer. He put one hand on her shoulder and ripped open the buttons on her blouse with the other. He pulled her toward him.

Hallie pried opened the jaws of the rattlesnake's head she had kept hidden behind her. The fangs extended forward, in biting position. She slid her hands low, around and behind him.

"Just answer me this," she said. "Did you find Mitch?"

"Yep...we won't have to worry 'bout him no more."

Thad squeezed her suddenly and lowered his head, clumsily trying to kiss her breasts. Without hesitation, Hallie drove the snake's fangs into his back with all her might. She pushed hard on the venom sacks in front of the dead eyes.

Thad shrieked in pain and pulled away. The snake's head was stuck to his back. Writhing and spinning violently, he shook it off. "You crazy bitch!" he screamed. "I'll kill you dead!"

As he turned to face Hallie, he saw his knife in her hand. Despite her terror, she looked dangerous. He was sure she would use it on him if she got the chance. The pain in his back continued to grow. He had no idea how much poison he had gotten. Barehanded, he was afraid he could not win

132

a fight with her. So he kept his distance.

"You're not gettin' outta' here alive," he yelled, wild-eyed and contorted from the bite. "I'm the only one who knows this place. When I get my gun, you're done for!"

Thad started toward the truck for his shotgun. Hallie Shugart turned and ran in the opposite direction. She knew her only chance was to put distance between them. She weaved through the trees, ignoring the brush and thorn vines. Hallie outdistanced him to a large thicket of fetterbush and grape vines along a stream bank. Going to her hands and knees, she crawled into the densest part of the thicket and hid.

Thad hunted her along the edge of the creek, waiting for her to make a sound. He knew the shotgun would be of little use if he followed her into the heavy brush. A covey of quail burst from the cover in front of him. Startled, he pulled the trigger, sending a blast of lead into a nearby tree. Hallie set the knife down and pulled herself into a tight ball.

After searching the length of the brush, Thad knew he wasn't going to find her. He backed away from the thicket a few paces. Lowering the gun, he fired volley after volley of buckshot into the bushes. Hallie bit down on her lip to quash a sudden pain. When the gunfire stopped, Thad began screaming.

"You come outta' there or I'm gonna' burn you out! You hear me?"

Hallie stayed put. If he started a fire there would be smoke. Smoke would be good cover for an escape...

Thad frantically searched his pockets for the lighter, not remembering he had dropped it in the fire he had set earlier.

"Damn!...Well...you 'kin rot in there!" he yelled. Then he picked up the shotgun and fired his last shell into the brush.

Hallie waited a full twenty minutes after she heard Thad leave before she allowed herself a deep breath. Her heart was still pounding. A trickle of blood and sweat was dripping from her chin, but she did not feel badly hurt. The buckshot had ripped the vegetation all around her. A slug had grazed the back of her head. It had removed some scalp but left her skull in one piece. After taking stock of her wound, she slowly crawled toward the edge of the thicket. Thad Henry was gone.

CHAPTER XIII

For the first half of the race, The Alligator had gone off without a hitch. Other than dealing with the dust and rising temperature, the competitors were having a good time. Then things started getting strange.

First, their gas cans weren't full like they should have been. Occasionally, a competitor will pirate gas from someone else, so most of the riders figured that must have been what happened. What came next was less easy to explain. As they entered the last loop of the race, the course just seemed to end. Their mileage charts and computers said that they had another twenty miles to cover. But there were no arrows. Instead, they found two signs hand painted on heavy cardboard. They read: "Save The Alligators", and "Handbags Are Murder".

More and more riders were arriving at the impasse. Nobody knew where the course was. Some raced about, trying to find it. All they found was the scorched woods left by the fire. One by one they gave up and went back to the last checkpoint to see what the workers there might know.

Several miles away, a frightened horse was careening down a trail. Mel Coburn was hanging on for dear life, trying to regain control. When the horse had bolted from the truck, the saddle had spun partway around the animal. Mel was flapping alongside, brush tearing at his face every time he tried to see ahead. The wound on his forehead had opened up again. It was bleeding into his eyes. He was finally able to pull himself on top of the horse. But now he was riding bareback.

He pulled back on the reins. The horse ducked its head and tried to throw him. Mel gave up trying to slow it down. He would let it run itself out. The jolting gallop was making his head pound in agony. It wasn't doing his testicles much good either. Through his blurred vision he could see that the trail was about to leave the woods. As he got closer to the opening, he saw people standing on either side. They appeared to have weapons pointed at him.

Suddenly, something hit him squarely between the eyes. He felt a stinging pain. Now he had lost all vision. He grabbed his face and felt a thick liquid. He thought it was blood from a gunshot wound. Losing his balance, Mel started to slide down the horse's flank. Its neck was too lathered with sweat to hang on to. He crashed to the ground, tumbling like a rag doll.

"We got him!" one of the gunners said with glee.

Two men and one woman approached Mel.

"Do you think that fall hurt him?" one of the men asked.

"Naw, he's just shaken up. Anyway, it serves him right," said the woman. "Let's truss him up."

The three put down their paintball guns and tied up their victim. Mel Coburn was groggy and confused. These people must have mistaken him for someone else, he thought. He started to explain who he was, and tried to tell them about Hallie. But the woman pulled out duct tape and slapped a length of it over his mouth.

"This will shut you up," she said triumphantly. "That's not real blood. We shot you with red paint, so settle down!" She turned to her comrades.

"You two get his horse...it's time he tasted freedom!"

Mel suddenly recognized her shrill voice. It was the woman from the truck stop.

The men caught Mel's horse and brought it back. They took off the saddle and bridle.

"You're free now!" the woman said.

The horse stood there, breathing hard.

"Go on, run...live as God intended!" she continued.

The horse put its head down and bit off some grass. One of the men walked up to the animal and slapped it on the rump. The horse startled, broke into a trot and disappeared into the woods.

"May you never carry another hunter!" the woman shouted after him.

They turned disgustedly back to Mel. Picking him up, they loaded him into the back of their pickup truck. Then they pulled a military style body bag around him and zipped him in. Small air holes were punched in the plastic.

"Now you can feel what it's like to be a corpse," the woman sneered.

Mel was beginning to believe the whole world had gone mad.

CHAPTER XIV

A lone red ant was following the trail laid down by a previous scouting party. It ended at a very large object. At first the ant just tested the object with its feelers, keeping its feet on the ground. Whatever it was, it was organic, probably edible. Finally, it used its hooked feet to climb straight up one side. The ant kept crawling until it could go no higher. As it spun around to survey its find, it felt the object move slowly and rhythmically. It was alive. The only thing to do was to kill it. The ant planted its feet, grabbed a jawfull of skin and drove its stinger deep into the fleshy hill.

A pain message made its way down intricate nerve pathways to the victim's subconscious. It called for a reaction to this unwelcome stimulus.

Rusty came to and crushed the ant on his nose.

He squinted at the bright sky as he opened his eyes. His head was throbbing. He rolled onto one shoulder to look around. There were bushes on all sides. It took him a while to realize he was at The Alligator. Then he remembered the fight with his cousin and wondered where he had gone.

As he rose to his knees and tried to clear his head, a wave of nausea overcame him. He lost what little was in his stomach. Resting his forehead against the ground, he spit to get rid of the sour taste in his mouth.

Slowly getting to his feet, he saw the gas truck. There were a couple of dozen riders around it getting refueled and waiting for their scheduled restart. He staggered to the truck and looked around for something to drink. He found a half filled water bottle and drank most of it. The rest he poured over his head. The noise of the bikes was making his headache worse. He stuck his fingers in his ears. The riders looked at him as though he was some drunken vagrant. Rusty got in the driver's side of the truck. The key was gone. He collected himself, then got out and started down the dirt road that led back to the campground.

The trip back promised to be long and hot. Rusty stopped to rest several times in what little shade there was along the road. As he came around a bend, he saw a cloud of dust coming toward him. As it got closer, he could see that it was a pickup truck. Behind it he could just make out another vehicle. One with a flashing blue light.

He decided to stand behind a nearby tree until they passed. The truck sped by him, tailgate banging open against the cable stays. It braked hard for the turn. As it fishtailed around the curve, a large parcel fell out of the back. It was wrapped in black plastic. The pursuing car veered, ran over the end of the object and kept after the truck.

Rusty McInster stayed behind the tree until they were out of sight. Then he walked to the road, to the jettisoned object. Kneeling cautiously next to it, he unzipped the bag and pulled it aside. The sight of the man's bloody face made Rusty jump back. The stranger was soaked in sweat, unconscious.

Rusty removed the ropes from the man. He dragged Mel Coburn into the shade. When he ripped the duct tape off, the man moved a bit. Rusty tried to get him to talk.

Mel felt his head being moved from side to side. A thin voice was calling to him. It seemed very distant. Slowly the voice grew louder, and he realized that someone was slapping him on the cheeks.

"Cut it out," he said weakly.

"You okay?" Rusty asked.

"Do I look okay?"

"You need a doctor."

Mel gradually propped himself up on his elbows.

"Where am I?"

"On an old cattle ranch we run races on."

"I figured that much. How far to get help?"

"About three miles. I could go and call for an ambulance. Hey, why were you tied up like that?"

"I'm not sure myself. Anyway, forget about me...there's a young lady that needs help, out in the woods."

"What's wrong with her?"

"She's being held captive by a maniac. I'm afraid he's going to hurt her...he may have already."

"Who is she?"

"Her name is Hallie Shugart."

Rusty sat back on his haunches to think about what he had just heard.

"Did the man have short reddish hair, sort of like mine?"

"Yeah, he did," Mel said suspiciously. "How did you know?"

"He's my cousin...I think he's gone out of his mind."

"I can confirm that," Mel said, touching his forehead gingerly. "But who are you?"

"Rusty...Rusty McInster."

"I'm Mel Coburn. We're no use sitting here, let's get some help."

"Where's he holding her?"

"At an old shack...probably a hunt camp."

"I think I know the place, it's not too far from here, over that way," Rusty pointed southeast.

Mel stood up and nearly fell over. "Something's wrong with my foot, it feels sprained."

"You got clipped by a sheriff's car. You're lucky he didn't kill you."

Mel grimaced and took a deep breath as he tested his foot. "We better get going."

"You take this road back to the campground. I'm gonna' find my cousin."

"Okay, but be careful, he's armed."

"He's almost always armed," Rusty said.

The two started walking in opposite directions. Rusty turned around and hollered to Mel; "When you call the cops, better tell them they're after Thad Henry. He's a murderer."

Mel stood and stared at the retreating form. "What have I gotten her into?" he asked himself as he turned and started toward the campground again.

CHAPTER XV

Hallie Shugart moved carefully as she made her way back toward the old hunt camp. If Mel was bringing help, he would return to the shack. She figured Thad would be off seeking medical treatment for the snake bite, or maybe dying from it. She took an indirect route, circling the area, looking things over from a distance. She froze when she saw Thad's old truck parked in the same spot as before. Hallie edged closer. She saw no trace of him. As she passed behind the truck, she saw that the motorcycle was gone.

After satisfying herself that nobody was there, Hallie approached the vehicle. The hood was up. Some mechanical problem. She figured Thad had taken the bike to go find a doctor. She wondered how he would explain a snake bite in the middle of his back. It would certainly make it easier for the police to track him down. She almost allowed herself some satisfaction. It vanished when she remembered what he had said about Mitch.

She looked in the truck and was surprised

to see the keys in the ignition. She got in and tried to start it. There was a clicking sound and a low growl as the engine barely turned over. But it wouldn't start. The battery was nearly dead.

In front of the truck the trail went down a small incline. Hallie thought if she could get the truck moving down the hill, she could start it by throwing it into gear. She closed the hood, then got back in and found neutral. Turning the key to the on position, she pumped the gas a few times and straightened the wheel. As she stepped out to push the truck, she remembered her own keys. They were under an old seat cushion on the floor of the cabin.

Hallie hurried into the shack's dim interior. When her eyes adjusted to the dark, she found the cushion and retrieved her keys. As she straightened up, she heard a twig break outside. Someone was walking toward the shack. Her heart quickened as she crouched in a corner. "Please be help," she whispered to herself. She moved closer to the wall, careful not to disturb the scattered beer cans. Hallie unconsciously rearranged her torn blouse to cover herself. There was a small crack between the boards of the wall. Hallie put her eye to it and peered out. At first she saw nothing. Then, just above the nearest palmettos, she caught a quick glimpse of a someone approaching. The blood seemed to freeze in her veins when she saw the man. Thad had returned to finish her off!

Hallie struggled to keep calm. Maybe he didn't know she was there, she thought. Maybe he had just come back for his truck. But then he would see that she had been there. She quietly finished sliding her truck keys into her pocket. Then, with equal stealth, she slid the hunting knife from its place under her belt.

Suddenly, the truck door banged shut. Hallie stifled a gasp and crouched lower. She listened intently as the footsteps came closer and closer. Her hand tightened on the knife handle. She heard him slowly coming up the steps. His dark figure appeared in the doorway. Hallie could feel the walls closing in on her.

Wild with fear, she rushed toward the door. As she swung the knife up, Hallie screamed at the top of her lungs.

"LEAVE ME ALONE!"

It was suddenly quiet. Hallie was horrified to see that the knife blade had disappeared into the man's gut. She looked up at his face. His eyes and mouth were wide open, locked in a silent scream. It was Rusty McInster. He staggered backward and fell down the steps. Hallie stared at the bloody knife in her hand, then at Rusty.

Throwing the knife down, she rushed to him. "Oh my God! Rusty! I didn't know it was you! There was a man...he was after me...I thought you..."

Rusty looked up at her and gasped for breath, "I know...my cousin Thad...I...was looking for him."

"We've got to get you some help," Hallie said, looking at the wound. "The race is going on, right?"

"Yeah."

"Then there should be an ambulance at the campground. Do you know how to get there?"

"Yeah."

"Okay, I'm going to try and stop the bleeding. Then maybe I can start the truck. Don't worry, you'll be alright," she said, trying to convince herself.

Hallie prayed that the knife had not hit any major organs or arteries. She knew that the visible flow of blood could be deceiving. He could be bleeding to death internally.

She decided to try and pack the wound and get some pressure on it. With the knife, she cut a piece of her blouse off and crouched down next to him.

"This might hurt."

She wadded up the cloth and pressed it against the wound. The blood kept flowing. Hallie gritted her teeth and pushed hard on the center of the makeshift dressing. Rusty moaned as it slid into the wound. She undid his belt and refastened it across the now saturated cloth. The flow of blood nearly stopped.

Hallie got up and ran to the truck. She decided to try the ignition once more. To her surprise, this time the engine cranked. She floored the gas pedal to keep it running. The truck jerked forward as she pushed in the clutch and jammed the transmission into low gear. She drove to where Rusty lay. Every time she took her foot off the gas, the engine threatened to die. Quickly, she grabbed one of the rocks from the fire pit and placed it on the pedal. The engine roared as she made her way to Rusty.

"Put your weight on me," she said as she took his arm. "Let's get you up on the seat."

Rusty grimaced as he strained to get to his feet. Hallie pulled his arm over her shoulder and guided him into the truck. She shut the passenger door, then ran around the truck and jumped in.

"Which way?" she asked.

"Go right, then take the first left. When it leaves the woods, go right until the power lines... I'll tell you where to go when we get there."

As she started off, Rusty slumped over in the seat. He tried to use his arms to keep the weight off his stomach.

"You better lie down," Hallie said. She put her arm around him and slid him closer. She rested his head in her lap.

"If I'm going too fast, just let me know."

"Don't slow down!"

Rusty noticed the blood on Hallie.

"Are you hurt? There's blood down the side of your face."

"Your cousin took a shot at me, but I'm all right. I can't tell you how sorry I am..."

"Don't feel sorry for me...I had this coming."

"What?"

"Thad killed Mark on account of me," he blurted out. "At least at first it was...but he lied to me...I didn't know he was going to do it, I swear."

"What are you talking about? What did you have to do with Mark?" Hallie's emotions began to boil over. She felt like she was falling backwards into a recurring nightmare.

"Thad offered to help me to...to...see if you and I could get together. I was crazy about you from the first time I saw you. I was so jealous of Mark...I know it was wrong, but I couldn't help it." He paused and winced in pain as they went over some rough road. "You see," he said slowly, "Thad had been staying with me for a while and he said he would help with Mark. But he told me he was only gonna' scare him off...he never said he would hurt him. I put Mark on the first row during sign up. Thad warned me not to pre-ride the section. But I didn't know about the wire, I swear."

149

Hallie let the tears run down her face. Rusty felt them landing on his cheek.

"I'm the one who should be sorry," he said. "I thought I could trust him. If I'd known what he was gonna' do, I woulda' stopped him...none of this would have happened."

Hallie didn't want to think about it any more.

"Do you know what's happened to Mitch?"

"I saw him this morning...on his bike."

"You did? Where?"

Hallie took her foot off the gas. Rusty braced himself against the dash as the truck suddenly slowed.

"At the gas stop."

"Was he okay?"

"He was when I saw him. But Thad and I were arguing and he sort of knocked my lights out. I don't know what happened after that...until I found this guy that fell out of a truck who told me where you were."

Hallie felt a glimmer of hope for Mitch.

"Did the man who told you where I was have a big gash on his forehead."

"Yeah, he had blood all over him...but I think he was okay. He went back to the camp for help."

Hallie turned onto the power line easement. Ahead, a group of vehicles were approaching.

CHAPTER XVI

As he walked toward the campground, Mel Coburn's strength vanished. The sun beat down on him as he struggled through the soft sand. It seemed like it took two steps to move one step forward. And the injured foot wouldn't take all his weight. Worse, he couldn't catch his breath. It reminded him of a time in the north Florida woods when his horse had bolted after he dismounted to relieve himself. He had to walk all the was back to the highway. The eight mile hike had left him dazed and dehydrated, but he had made it. He was too embarrassed to ever admit that the horse had spooked when he had broken wind. But back then nobody's life depended on him. Nor had he been bludgeoned by a madman, trapped in a body bag and hit by a car.

The sweat was pouring down his face, bringing with it rivulets of blood and red paint. When he wet his lips, he could taste both. It was making him nauseous. He struggled on, determined to reach the campground. The heat seemed to grow more intense. After a while he became aware that he had stopped sweating. As he marched on, he began to feel as though he was burning up. His balance was starting to fail. Finally, he saw the campground. It seemed to swim in front of him. He passed through rows of parked trucks, trailers and motorhomes. Nobody seemed to take notice of him. He made his way to a group of people under a large tree. Mel opened his mouth to speak, but no words came out. The group of people stared at him in shock, then two of them grabbed him by the arms and set him down. Mel heard one of them shout: "Call the ambulance!"

Charlie Dorge was pulling into the opposite end of the campground. He had lost the chase with the pickup truck when the sand road had gotten too soft for his squad car. He was steaming mad. First, he had taken the wrong entrance road getting onto the property. Second, he had no idea why the pickup truck had taken flight when he pulled up to ask directions. It was possible that Mossback was in the truck, and now he had gotten away. To add insult to injury, the rough chase had knocked his radio out. Then he saw Mel Coburn being carried to the ambulance.

By the time the detective pushed through the crowd around Mel, the medics had loaded him up and were giving him emergency treatment for heat stroke.

"Who is this guy?" Dorge demanded of one attendant.

"His identification says he's Melvin Coburn, from Tallahassee. He keeps babbling about a murderer, and a girl in trouble. I'm afraid he's pretty delirious."

"Let me in there."

The detective squeezed past the attendant and knelt in a puddle next to Mel. They had packed ice around him to bring his temperature down. It was quickly melting in the ambulance. Charlie Dorge patted him on the cheek.

"Hey buddy, wake up!"

Mel Coburn opened his eyes. He feverishly started talking. "Save the girl...murderer's out there...got her...Rusty...the old hunt camp."

"Slow down...who's out there?"

"Hallie...Rusty...murderer..."   Suddenly Mel's eyes rolled back and he was silent.

"That's enough!" the attendant cut in. "We're heading to the hospital... Now!"

Dorge reluctantly climbed out of the ambulance. Sirens wailing, it headed toward the highway.

The detective turned to several of the club members that had gathered at the ambulance.

"You guys know anything about an old hunting camp out here?"

"Sure," Joe Brown said. "It's been here

153

since we were kids...why?"

"Take me there."

"Right now?"

"According to that guy in the ambulance, Rusty McInster is holding Hallie Shugart out there with the intent to kill her."

"Rusty?" Joe said with disbelief. "You can't be serious."

"Are you going to cooperate or am I going to have to arrest you for obstruction of justice?"

"Okay, okay, take it easy...we'll take you there."

"That's better."

"But are you sure about Rusty. I don't think he'd..."

"Let's get going. I don't want to prove you wrong the hard way."

Joe motioned for the others. "Let's go see what he's talking about. It looks like we've lost the last loop anyway."

The detective followed the four motorcycles out of the campground. After a few miles they emerged onto the powerline easement. Ahead, they saw a beat up old pickup truck approaching fast. They pulled over to the side of the road. Hallie Shugart drove up to them and stopped. Charlie Dorge got out of his car. She got out to meet him, waving her hands toward the truck.

154

"Rusty's in there....he's hurt...he has..."

She cut herself short when the detective suddenly drew his gun.

"You got Rusty McInster in there?"

"Yes, I accidentally stabbed him...he needs help."

"You stabbed him?" The detective pushed her to the side and pointed his revolver into the truck cab.

"Freeze!" he shouted.

Rusty looked up at him helplessly.

"I need help," he said, holding out one bloody palm.

The detective took his handcuffs from his belt. He leaned into the truck and put his knee on Rusty's neck. Then he grabbed Rusty's arm and snapped one end of the cuffs on it.

"Hey!" Hallie shouted. "You're hurting him. He has a stab wound..."

"You shut up!" Dorge snapped. "I'll handle him."

He finished handcuffing Rusty, then pulled him out of the truck.

"What are you doing?" Hallie asked. "Can't you see he's hurt?"

"Looks like you got him pretty good. From the looks of your blouse and that blood on your face, I'd say he got what he deserved."

"He's not the one..."

"The ambulance just left," Dorge interrupted. "Guess I'll have to get him to the hospital. You're coming along...I need a statement."

He loaded Rusty into the back of the squad car. Hallie took a step back.

"I want to stay here. Mitch is out here somewhere and I need to find him."

"I'm real sorry that you two keep losing each other...but like I said, you're going with me!"

The detective took hold of her wrist and squeezed. He pulled her toward his car. Hallie pulled back, then dug her nails into his wrist with her free hand. Dorge quickly pulled a leather covered object from his coat and brought it down sharply on the back of her hand. The blackjack made a smacking sound as it hit. Hallie pulled her hand back. The pain was excruciating, but she wasn't going to give him any satisfaction.

"You bastard!"

"Come along quietly, before I have to arrest you too." he said, continuing to pull on her wrist.

During the scuffle, Jerry Cochran, a long-time dirt biker and good friend of Mitch Clanton, had been uneasily edging closer to the detective. He didn't like what was going down, nor how the detective was behaving. When he hit Hallie, Jerry saw red. At six-four and two-forty, he was a force to be reckoned with. Now he closed on Charlie

156

Dorge from behind and locked his arms around him, pinning the detective's arms to his sides. Hallie pulled free.

"Let go of me!" Dorge demanded.

Jerry squeezed him harder and lifted him off the ground.

Sam ripped off his helmet. "Jerry, what are you doing?"

"Nobody should hit a girl like that!" Jerry said through clenched teeth. "This guy needs to learn some manners."

"Can't argue with that. But he's the law, you can't just suffocate him." Sam noticed the detective was having trouble breathing.

"If Hallie wants to stay here, I think she should be able to," Jerry said. "Hallie, what do you know about Mitch?"

"All I know is that Rusty's cousin said he did something to him. Then Rusty said that he saw him on his bike at the gas stop. So he's out here somewhere."

Hallie stood in front of the detective. She was rubbing her aching hand.

"Listen up, big shot," she said. "Very likely there's a man seeking medical help for a rattlesnake bite to the middle of his back. That man is Rusty's cousin, his name is Thad Henry. According to Rusty, he set the wire that killed Mark. He held me and Mel Coburn prisoner since yesterday. He almost killed both of us...you getting all this.?"

The detective's face was red with rage.

"Rusty can fill you in on some of the details. I'll be glad to make a statement later. But right now finding Mitch is more important. I'd appreciate it if you'd get your head out of your ass long enough to get some deputies out here to help us."

She took the revolver from the holster on Dorge's chest. She also picked up the blackjack he had dropped.

"Sam, put these in a safe place. I don't think we can trust the detective to cooperate."

Sam sighed as he took the weapons. He put them in his fanny pack and zipped it shut.

She returned to the deputy and relieved him of his key ring. Then Hallie helped Rusty out of the rear seat and removed the handcuffs. Sam took his arm and helped her load him into the front of the squad car. As an afterthought, she walked around to face Dorge and put the cuffs on his wrists. She squeezed them hard enough to bite into his skin.

"Let's see how you like it."

Dorge started to curse at her, but Jerry tightened his hold again and the detective went silent.

"Put him in the back," Hallie said. "I think we can lock him in back there. Who wants to drive Rusty to the hospital?"

"I reckon I'm already in the most trouble, so I'll take him," said Jerry.

"Can I use your bike?" Hallie asked him.

"Sure. Take my riding gear too."

They shoved the detective in the back and shut the self-locking door. Hallie gave Jerry the keys and started to put on his riding gear. Jerry Cochran spun the squad car around and drove off. They could all hear Dorge screaming at him from the caged rear compartment. About a quarter mile away, they saw the car stop. Jerry leaped out, walked deliberately to the back of the cruiser and opened the trunk. He then yanked open a rear door and dragged Dorge out. Snatching him off the ground, Jerry tossed him in the trunk and slammed it shut.

"Oh, Christ!" Sam lamented. It's going to take us a while to raise Jerry's bail money.

"Where should we start looking for Mitch?" Hallie asked.

"Last night we were out here looking for you. We found your truck and pulled it off a log. My guess is that Mitch would have started there," Wayne said.

"Okay, you guys lead the way."

The five riders headed north. As they traveled, the breeze freshened and the humidity rose. Storm clouds were building behind them.

CHAPTER XVII

Mitch followed the knobby tire tracks to a far corner of the property. They ended near a gate at a dirt road that accessed some nearby ranchettes. He could see from the marks in the sand that the rider had loaded the bike into a vehicle. Instead of leaving the property, the driver had gone south, down a narrow woods trail. Mitch knew that Rusty owned a pickup truck. He turned south and followed the new tracks.

Mitch was not feeling well. The back of his right hand was completely blistered and his lungs had gotten worse. He kept coughing up a thin pink mucous. Each cough made his broken rib stick into tender muscles. He hoped that he would soon find what he was after.

The tracks continued deep into the forest. Once in a while he would stop to listen. All he heard was the racket of cicadas noisily celebrating their emergence from the earth.

It was becoming hard to follow the tire tracks. The grass in the road had absorbed the weight of the vehicle without leaving much trace. Mitch strained to see if the driver had taken any of the side trails that laced these woods. As he stopped, looking intently at the trail, he heard a motorcycle approaching. Glancing up, he saw a bike cross the trail in front of him and disappear. Mitch recognized Rusty's bike and riding gear. He stomped his KTM into gear and took off in pursuit. The other bike had a good head start. But Mitch knew he was faster than the younger, less experienced rider. At least when he wasn't busted up. The pain in his body kept building as he picked up speed. He pushed it aside and concentrated on closing the distance between them.

He started thinking about what he would say to Rusty once he caught him. Mitch was in no condition to fight. But Rusty wouldn't know that. He hoped he could reason with him. But he was prepared to do whatever it took to learn where Hallie was.

Mitch slowly gained on the other bike. He began to pull alongside. The other rider was weaving from side to side. Mitch motioned him to stop. Suddenly they collided. The next thing Mitch knew, he was bouncing through the palmettos. He came to a rough stop, barely able to stay upright. He pulled angrily back on the trail and picked up the chase.

The other rider was traveling faster now.

But his path was erratic, like a rank amateur. Mitch couldn't understand why he couldn't keep the bike pointed straight. The distance between the two machines began to narrow. Mitch knew this trail. It went to the old rock mine and turned sharply west. He hoped Rusty knew this. Unless he slowed down, he would never make the turn. Mitch decided he would try to knock him over to stop him. The best way would be to "stuff" him in a turn. He would try to take out Rusty's front wheel. It was a dirty tactic, but Mitch was beyond caring if Rusty got hurt. There was only one corner to go before the quarry.

Mitch gave his bike full throttle as they entered the last turn. He would use Rusty's bike as a pivot point. But at the last second, the other bike again lurched into his. Their footpegs and handlebars became tangled. Now they were flying down the trail toward the pit together. Mitch couldn't get to his brakes with Rusty's bike in the way. "Stop!" Mitch yelled as loud as he could. At first the other rider seemed not to comprehend. The sight of the cliff brought him to his senses. He slammed on the brakes.

The two bikes parted and fell. Now they were sliding sideways. The ground began to slope down near the edge of the pit. Mitch pushed himself free of his bike. He rolled onto his stomach, trying to dig his fingers and boots into the hard surface. At any second he expected to be free-falling into the mine. As the slope steepened, jutting rocks bruised his legs and chest. He came to a jolting stop. Some seconds later he heard two splashes below. Cautiously, he looked around.

Below him and to one side he saw the other rider. He too had stopped on the steep slope, closer to the drop. A single rock had saved him from the long plunge into the water. He was hanging on with both hands. His legs were dangling in space.

"Help me!" the man pleaded.

Mitch was suddenly puzzled.

"Rusty?"

"No, I ain't Rusty."

"Who are you?"

"His kin...from the gas stop! Help me! I cain't swim!"

Mitch could see the whites of his eyes through his goggles. The man was obviously scared stiff.

"Where's Rusty?"

"I don't know...Help me!."

"I'll try. Hang on."

Mitch began to pull himself sideways until he was directly over Thad Henry. He found that he could cut footholds into the slope by kicking with the steel toes of his boots. Slowly he worked his way down. The effort was draining him. At last he was just above and to one side of the rock. Mitch knew he had to calm down the other man.

"What's your name?" Mitch asked.

"Thad...Thad Henry. Yer Mitch, right?"

"Yes. I'm going to try to help you up. But we've got to take it slow."

"Okay."

"I've made some footholds over here. I'll get your left hand and try to pull you over. See if you can get your foot in this lowest notch."

"Don't let me fall!"

"Nobody's going to fall. We just need to take it easy."

Mitch secured his feet as best he could. Then he reached out with his left hand and found a crevice above Thad. He squeezed his fingers in as far as he could. By tightening his hand into a fist, it wedged tight in the crack.

"Here we go."

Mitch swung his right hand down and worked it under Thad's wrist.

"Don't knock me loose!"

"Calm down! Let your hand slide onto my hand. Then grip it for all your worth!"

Mitch watched Thad's gloved fingers slowly start to straighten, loosening their grip on the rock. He felt the man's weight start to pull on his arm. Their fingers locked around each other's hands. Mitch hoped Thad wouldn't make a mistake. If they both went into the quarry, they would likely drown. In his condition, Mitch was pretty sure he couldn't swim wearing heavy riding boots and knee braces.

Mitch steadied himself and pulled. "Lift yourself up with your other hand on the rock...I need all the help I can get!"

Thad slowly came up, until he was almost even with Mitch's knee. Without warning, Thad lost his grip on the rock. He lunged and caught Mitch's hand. Now his full weight was on it.

"Use your feet!" Mitch hollered through his pain. "Find a foothold!"

Mitch could hear Thad's boots scraping against the rocks. Then he felt blisters tearing.

CHAPTER XVIII

Hallie Shugart was having a hard time keeping up with the others. It wasn't that they were going fast. She just couldn't see very well. Jerry's large helmet wouldn't stay put. It kept sliding down over her eyes, pushing the goggles past her nose. She tried riding while holding the helmet with her left hand, but it was no good. She had to stop and try to fix it.

Hallie watched the others continue on, figuring she could catch up easy enough. She decided to take off Jerry's gloves and stuff them under the helmet to take up the excess space. Hallie veered off the trail as she came to a stop. It took about two minutes to jury rig the helmet. She never saw the cactus in front of her as she hurried to get back on the trail. For a while it was easy to follow the other bikes. There were no other tire tracks except theirs in the area. Then she came to an intersection. It was near where the enduro course had disappeared. There were motorcycle tracks everywhere. She couldn't tell which way they had gone, so she continued straight ahead. For some reason the bike was becoming hard to control. It was several minutes before she realized that the front tire was going flat.

As the tire went slowly down, the tracks she had been following turned around. She knew she'd been wrong about the others. They must have turned off at the intersection. Hallie stopped, exasperated with the front tire. As she tried to turn around, the front tire plowed sideways through the sand, coming half off the rim. She decided to limp the bike back to camp and get more help. As she and the bike made a wobbly retreat, she could have sworn she heard a horse whinny in the bushes. She shut off the bike. Walking quietly, she located Mel's horse. She saw that all its tack had been removed. Then she remembered the tow rope wrapped around Jerry's handlebar clamps. She took off his helmet, walked back for the rope, then returned to the horse.

"Easy, boy," she whispered soothingly. "You remember me...I'm not going to hurt you..."

The horse stared at her for a few moments, then went back to browsing on the wild blueberries. Hallie made a noose in the rope and slowly held her hand out to the animal. It lifted its nose to sniff her. She stroked the horse's forelock as she slid the rope over it.

"There you go...It's okay. What are you

doing way out here all by yourself?"

She looked back at the motorcycle. They could pick it up later. Besides, it would be easier to search for Mitch from horseback. She would be able to see and hear better.

Hallie had only ridden bareback once before. But that was on an ancient swayback mare. She remembered that her feet had almost touched the ground. But this animal was an athlete. Without a proper bridle, she would have to be careful. After reassuring the horse, she jumped up on the left side. It broke into a trot as she pulled herself onto its back. Struggling, Hallie got a leg over and sat up. She leaned forward and took hold of the mane. The loose end of the rope was dragging on the ground, so she coiled it up in one hand. By pulling back on the rope and mane at the same time, she got him slowed to a walk. Hallie managed to turn the horse around the way she had come. But when they got to the motorcycle, the horse stopped.

"Come on, boy, that's not going to bother you."

The horse refused to go near the bike. Hallie could tell he was getting jumpy. Not wanting to dismount, she turned him around.

"Okay...we'll go your way."

As they continued, Hallie could see rain falling in the distance. Once in a while there was a rumble of thunder. The trail went on for some time.

Finally it crossed another trail. She could clearly see motorcycle tracks leading to the right. Hallie turned and followed.

At the end of the same trail, two men were fighting for their lives. Mitch was trying to reach the next foothold. It was his only hope of saving the stranger dangling from his hand. But his strength was almost gone. With one desperate tug, he pushed off and raised his left foot up the cliff. Just as the toe of his boot made the foothold, the blistered skin on his hand peeled back. In an instant, Thad was falling. His hand burning fiercely, Mitch made a grab for him. Too late. All he could do was cling to the rocks and listen to the other man scream as he fell. The sound echoed across the quarry for long seconds. Then came the splash.

Mitch slumped sideways, onto the rock next to him. He looked out over the edge. Through the sheen of gasoline on the clear water he could see two motorcycles. Between them was Thad Henry. He was fighting his helmet strap with gloved hands. Mitch watched in fascinated horror as the man struggled. Thad kept sinking. Silt began to rise around the drowning man. For a moment Mitch thought about going in after him. But he knew it was hopeless. He slowly lost sight of Thad as muddy billows rose from the bottom. A few more bubbles broke the surface. Then nothing.

The effort to save the other man had left Mitch in bad shape. He could barely breathe. The mucous he coughed up was now stringy and red. His hand hurt so bad he chewed his lower lip bloody trying to cope with it.

Hallie had heard Thad Henry scream. She let the horse speed up to a gallop. Soon she came to the quarry. All she could see were the skid marks.

"Anyone there?" she yelled.

Someone was coughing. Hallie got off the horse and hurried toward the pit. She repeated the question.

Mitch took a breath and strained to speak. "Down here," he said.

"Mitch! Is that you?"

"Yes...Hallie...you're okay?"

"I'm okay. What about you? Can you climb up?"

"I'm stuck here...can you get help?"

"I'm not sure how to get back. Are you hurt?"

"I can't climb...no strength...pretty banged up."

"What's wrong?"

"Not sure...lungs not working...there was a fire...burned my hand"

"How far down to the water?"

"Good sixty feet...never make it.

"I could come down and help you up."

"No...too dangerous...no room."

"I have some rope, Maybe I can pull you up."

"How?"

"I've got a horse. Maybe I can use him."

"Okay..."

Hallie brought the horse toward the edge and removed the rope. She tossed one end down to Mitch.

"Can you reach it?"

"Move it left...okay...got it."

Hallie put a rock on her end of the rope. Then she brought the horse closer. She got the rope and opened the noose. She tried to put it over the animal's head, but it wouldn't reach.

"Mitch! Can you give me any slack?"

"No...hardly have enough."

Hallie tried to get the horse closer. It took one step, then two. Hallie threw the noose over its head just as it slipped on the rocks. The frightened animal reared back, snatching Hallie off the ground. Mitch wasn't prepared for the sudden pull. The rope burned into the palm of his good hand before he could let go. Hallie was desperate to keep the horse from running off. She grimly held onto the rope as it dragged her away from the edge. The animal finally calmed down. Hallie tried to walk it back to the quarry. It was no use.

171

"Mitch! The horse is spooked. This isn't going to work." Suddenly a thought hit her.

"Wayne said you guys got my truck unstuck. If I can find it I can pull you out that way."

"Good idea. It's not far...the way you came...take the second trail left...about a mile."

"Will you be alright?"

"I think so..."

"I'll be back as quick as I can."

Hallie mounted the horse and grabbed its mane. "You're going to have to cooperate!" she said sternly. She spurred it gently into a gallop. The steady rhythm of the horse made Hallie feel like she was being timed. For a while she couldn't stop crying. Mitch was alive.

CHAPTER XIX

Sam Braselton and the others couldn't find Hallie. One minute she was behind them, then she just seemed to vanish. They backtracked and searched the nearby trails. All they found was Jerry's motorcycle. And hoofprints.

"What do you guys make of this?" Sam asked.

Paul was inspecting the front tire. "Looks like she got tired of riding on a flat. Wonder who was on the horse that picked her up?"

"Don't know, but from the looks of that sky, I hope they're headed back to camp."

"Looks like they went that way," Joe said. "Maybe a couple of us should check it out."

"Good idea. You and Wayne keep looking for Mitch. Paul and I will follow the horse. We'll meet up at the north canal where we built that bridge crossing."

The first raindrops began to fall as they started out. Before long the rain was coming down in sheets. They crouched down on their motorcycles, letting their helmet visors catch the worst of it. Joe and Wayne were taking a trail that circled north, near the back entrance to the property. They knew the area well and kept up a fast pace. Lightning was starting to crack around them. They searched for several miles and found no trace of Mitch. Joe Brown stopped to clear his goggles. Wayne pulled alongside.

"Hope this rain quits," said Wayne. "I'm freezing my ass off."

"Yeah," Joe said. "But we should cover this area. 'Course, with any luck, we'll find Mitch back at camp."

"Hope so."

"There's a jeep road to the left up here that was part of the course. It cuts over to the trail Sam and Paul are on. Let's take it to make sure it gets searched."

"Okay."

As they started down the new path, the rain slacked off. They were about half way to the other end of the trail when Joe noticed something in the middle of the road. He wiped his goggles and saw it was a woman. He signaled to Wayne to slow down. As they got closer, the woman didn't move. She was holding the end of a rope that went up into the trees. Puzzled, they braked to a stop in front of her. She turned suddenly and ran in the opposite direction, still holding the rope. They heard a commotion up above. As they looked up, a large cargo net came down. The weight of it pinned them on their bikes. Before they could move, two young men and the woman were standing on the edges of the net, holding weapons.

"What the hell are you doing?" Joe yelled at them.

They began circling the trapped riders, rapid firing paintballs at them.

"Cut it out!" Wayne hollered.

Joe let his bike fall over and tried to crawl out from under the net. One of the men jumped on him and clubbed him with his fists. Joe's helmet absorbed the pounding. He managed to get his feet braced and lunged against the man. They went sprawling, each trying to strike the other through the mesh. Joe got one arm through the net. He grabbed hold of the man's neck and held him to the ground. The other man threw down his paintball gun and joined in the fight.

In the commotion, no one noticed the two other motorcycles coming fast down the trail. Paul got there first. He aimed his bike to the side of the net. When he was in range, he leaped off his bike. As the second man turned to look, Paul tackled him at speed. The top of his helmet crashed into the man's face, breaking his nose. They tumbled across the net. Paul ended up on top of him, holding his face in the dirt. The woman rushed at Paul, preparing to fire a paint ball at point-blank range. A gunshot split the air above their heads.

"Hold it!" Sam bellowed.

They all turned to see Sam stopped a short distance away. He had pulled out the detective's revolver. The smoking barrel was pointed at the sky. The woman dropped her gun and ran. Sam let her go.

Sam walked over to Joe. "He's turning blue, Joe, I think you can let go now."

Joe kept his grip. "You had enough?"

"Nnnnnngh," the man groaned.

"I'll take that as a yes." Joe released him.

Sam kicked the man in the thigh. "You...get these two out of the net...now!"

The young man scrambled to pull the net back. Joe and Wayne were soon free. Paul was still sitting on his man.

"I want some answers," Sam continued. "Just what are you doing here?"

The man with the broken nose spoke up. "We're on a mission."

"Don't tell them anything!" the other said.

"They're going to find out!"

"What mission?" Sam cut in.

"To stop the killing of wildlife, you know...the alligators."

"Killing alligators?" Joe asked. "Are you the guys that wrote that letter to our club?"

"Yes."

"What gave you the idea that we were going to hunt alligators?"

"We saw it on the internet."

"What?"

"Yeah, on your web site," the other broke in.

Joe turned to Wayne. "Wayne, you set up our computer stuff. What's this about hunting alligators?"

"It was a joke. Remember last year when we pretended a bunch of riders got eaten during the race? I just put in there that this year they could even the score. I didn't think anyone besides riders would read it."

"Just these cockroaches," Paul interjected. "Are you the ones that took down our course arrows?"

"Yeah, Gwen told us we had to do anything we could to disrupt the hunt...or...whatever this is."

"Trust me, this event has nothing to do with hunting," Sam said.

"But Gwen said..."

"I think Gwen has taken a powder. How'd you guys get here?"

"Our pickup is in the bushes over there."

"Have you seen a guy by himself on a motorcycle."

"No."

"How about a young lady, maybe with someone else on a horse?"

"No. But we did set a horse free today."

"Let's run these guys in," Paul offered. "Maybe some jail time would make them think twice before pulling a shitty stunt like this again."

"Maybe so, but we still need to find Hallie and Mitch," Sam said. "We should pick up where we lost the hoofprints. Let's take these guys with us in their truck. Put two of the bikes in the back."

As they loaded up the bikes, another rain squall began. Sam and Paul made their captives ride in the back. Wayne and Joe fell in behind them. About a mile later they came upon the trail Hallie had taken.

"There's hoofprints heading toward the old quarry," Paul said. "Let's check it out."

CHAPTER XX

Hallie finally came to the trail that led to her truck. It was all she could do to slow the horse down and get it pointed in the right direction. As she entered the woods, a curtain of rain fell on them. There was a great flash of lightning. Hallie tightened her grip. The crash of thunder was deafening. The horse panicked and broke into a full out run. Hallie tried to hang on. The rain, mixed with the horse's sweat, was making things slippery. Hallie began sliding down the side of the animal. She hit the ground with her legs and tried running to keep up, but it was no use. Despite being dragged, she wouldn't let go of the rope. The thin nylon cut into her hands and the horse's neck. The horse finally had enough. He spun around, lowered his head and started yanking backwards. The noose slid up and pulled free from his neck. Hallie skidded to a stop, face down on the muddy trail. She looked up in time to see the horse's backside disappearing into the ozone spiked rain. She picked herself up. Her knees had taken a beating, but she

179

still had the rope. Running down the trail through the rain, she nearly ran past her own truck. She threw the rope in the back, got in and pulled out her keys. The truck started instantly. She hit the wipers, put it in gear and peeled out toward the quarry through the mud hole in front of her. The truck spun and slid, but made it through.

Within minutes she was at the pit. She backed the truck up as far as she dared. Hallie jumped out and ran to make sure Mitch was still there. He squinted up at her through the raindrops. With the noose over the trailer hitch, she again dropped the rope to Mitch. Now it was raining buckets.

"Tie yourself on!"

Mitch tied the rope around his chest, underneath his armpits.

"Okay."

"You ready?"

"I guess...go easy."

As the truck moved, the rope stretched. Taking his weight, it bit into Mitch's bruised muscles. He could see the rope sliding across the rock above him. It was being tested to its limit. Slowly he started up, suspended from an overhanging rock. The rope had found a notch that was being deepened by friction. When an old knot lodged there, Mitch quit going up.

"Hold it!" he tried to yell over the storm.

Hallie didn't hear him. The rope continued to stretch. With a snap it parted. Mitch felt a sting as it struck his neck. He banged into the rocks below, then became airborne. It felt better not being pulled. The fall was peaceful. Unexpectedly, he felt like a little kid again, enjoying the dizzy weightlessness. Dying wasn't going to be so bad after all, he thought. The water rushed up to meet him. It felt like concrete when he hit.

When the truck lurched forward, Hallie realized something had gone wrong. She jumped out and hurried to the quarry. The edge was too far away to see the water directly below. She quickly sat and unlaced her boots. Peeling off her jeans, she backed up, then raced for the edge and leaped. She was well clear of the wall on the way down. With her toes pointed, she cut cleanly into the water, touching the bottom twenty feet below the surface.

She burst up through the water. The pit danced with a million raindrops. Nearer to the wall, she saw bubbles.

Hallie swam to the spot and jackknifed toward down. With her eyes open, she could barely see the bottom before she got there. She searched frantically for Mitch. Her lungs felt like they were about to burst when she saw something white. A helmet. She grabbed it, locked one arm around his neck and kicked hard for the surface. She gasped for air as her head broke clear of the water. The gasoline slick burned her eyes as she looked for a place to go. There was a small ledge at the foot of the wall. Hallie swam for it. She had been trained in CPR, but never thought she would have to use it.

At the ledge, she pulled herself up into a sitting position. Locking her legs around his body, she unfastened the helmet. Thad Henry's head fell back into her lap. A small catfish squirmed out of his mouth and back into the water. Hallie stifled a scream. Horrified, she pushed the body away. The corpse gaped at her before sinking feet first. As she prepared to dive back in, there was a faint voice over the pounding rain.

Hallie shielded her eyes against the rain. "Mitch!...where are you?"

"Over here," he wheezed.

Through the mist, Hallie could see him holding onto a limb of a willow tree at the water's edge. In his other hand was his helmet. He was using it as a float. Hallie dove in and hurried to him. Blood was streaming from his nose.

"Mitch...thank God. I couldn't have taken it if you were...I mean..."

"It's okay...I was...going crazy looking for you...too."

"Did the fall hurt you?"

"Can't catch my breath...feel like I'm drowning."

"What should I do?"

"Get my boots off...weighing me down."

Hallie dove down and began undoing his boots. Once the buckles were loose, she yanked one off, accidentally pulling Mitch underwater. She helped him back to the surface, then carefully took off the other boot. Putting one arm around him, Hallie began swimming across the quarry to the other side, where she could see an old haul road angling down to the water. The pit was about a hundred yards across. Not a long swim for Hallie, but she went slowly, feeling Mitch wince when she pulled too hard. The bolts of lighting were coming closer together now. Echoing thunder rolled continuously back and forth between the rock walls above.

Halfway across the pit, she had a feeling they were not alone. A current of cooler water washed against the bare skin of her legs. Something big was swimming just beneath them. Hallie concentrated on the bank she had to reach, trying to block out everything else. She looked back to make sure Mitch was okay. That was when she saw the huge reptile behind them. Only a dark snout and pair of eyes were visible above the surface. Hallie knew by the distance between them that this was a large alligator, well over ten feet long. She tightened her grip on Mitch. Without losing a stroke, she whispered to him, "We've got a gator following us."

"I know...been watching him."

"What are we gonna' do?"

"Just...keep swimming...don't splash...he may just be curious. I'll let you know...if he closes in."

Hallie kept swimming for what seemed like hours. They were still forty feet from the bank when the reptile submerged.

"He's down..."

"Oh God, Mitch...is he going to get us?"

"If he attacks...save yourself, Hallie."

"No Mitch, we're in this together."

Just then her fingers struck something hard. She recoiled, then realized it was part of the abandoned haul road. Hallie scrambled to her feet, sliding Mitch up the incline. She pulled him out of the water. He couldn't stand.

Behind them the water suddenly boiled as the gator came partway up the slope. It arched its tail clear of the water and opened its mouth wide in a threat display.

"He's trying to scare us," Mitch said.

"It's working."

"Get a rock and hit him...don't get too close."

Hallie found a softball-sized rock and threw it. It went over the alligator's head. The huge animal opened it's mouth wider and hissed loudly.

She found another rock and let it fly. This one struck the side of its snout. The water seemed to explode as the gator spun around and disappeared into a sea of foam. The rain quickly erased all traces of the eleven foot reptile.

Mitch was grinning up at her. "Hallie Shugart...Alligator Slayer," he said weakly.

She had to make fists to keep her hands from shaking.

"I'm going to get my truck...I'll be right back."

Mitch was shivering from the rain. He just nodded.

Hallie scrambled up the steep road toward the top of the pit. To her dismay, the entire upper end had been blocked off with boulders. She searched for a way over the rocks. It was going to be difficult. She ran back to where Mitch was huddled.

"Mitch, the road is blocked. I'm not going to be able to get the truck down here. I'll go for help."

Mitch didn't respond. Hallie kneeled down next to him. He was looking very pale. She put her lips to his ear.

"Mitch?"

"Mmmmm...?"

"You've got to hang on for a little while...please...I need you." She kissed him, checked his pulse just to make sure, then headed back up.

The trip over the boulders was punishing. The rocks were slick from the rain. Hallie's fingers and toes were bloodied as she slipped and slid her way up. Near the top was a wide gap, forcing her to jump. She made it over, but split the skin badly under her big toe on the landing. She ran limping the rest of the way to her truck.

Realizing that she was half naked, Hallie fished a pair of shorts and a raincoat from a duffel bag behind the seat. She turned the truck around and started away from the quarry. Hallie knew only the general direction of the campground. Through the windshield wipers, the dirt road looked like a small river, flowing back toward the quarry. She worried that she hadn't pulled Mitch far enough from the rising water. Gripping the wheel harder, she picked up speed.

CHAPTER XXI

The terrain came in brief glimpses between the passes of the windshield wiper. Hallie Shugart leaned over the wheel to get a better view of the twisting trail. It didn't help much. The oncoming headlights were almost on her before she could react. She wrenched the wheel right. The truck slid off the narrow road, crashing through palmettos. The oncoming pickup fishtailed past as the driver tried to stop. Hallie caught a glimpse of Sam Braselton at the wheel.

She regained control of her truck and made it back on the jeep trail. Sam had stopped some distance behind her. He was coming back in reverse. Hallie jumped out and ran to the green truck. She yanked open the driver's door as Wayne and Joe pulled up on their bikes. While she was catching her breath, Sam motioned her to calm down.

"That was a close one," he said.

Hallie forced herself to take a deep breath. "I found Mitch! He's hurt pretty bad...we need to go get him!"

"Where is he?"

"In a rock quarry!"

"Go on, we'll follow you!"

On the way back to the pit, the rain let up as the clouds thinned. Hallie drove to the top of the haul road and stopped. Sam pulled alongside. They both got out and she led him to the blockade of boulders.

"Where is he?"

"Down there!" she pointed.

"Where?"

"At the bottom of the slope."

Sam jumped up on a nearby rock for a better look. He could hardly believe what he saw.

"Oh shit! He's down there alright, but he's got trouble...a big gator is trying to drag him in!"

"No!" Hallie cried, grabbing handfuls of her hair. She knew it would take some minutes to get down to Mitch. "We've got to do something ...quick!"

Sam picked up a rock and threw it in the direction of the gator. It landed hopelessly short. Then he remembered the revolver. He ran to the truck to get it. Paul Wedgefield was guarding the two young men. Joe and Wayne had dismounted and were walking toward Sam.

"Mitch is down there, but there's a gator that's got hold of him! I'm getting the pistol. You guys get down there as fast as you can. Leave your riding gear on, those rocks look bad!"

Joe and Wayne looked wide-eyed at each other, then bolted toward the incline. Sam fished under the seat for the stashed revolver. He knew it was too long a shot for a handgun, he would have to get much closer to use it effectively. To his surprise, his groping fingers closed around the long maple stock of a powerful rifle. He pulled it out. There were no bullets in the magazine .

"Hey!" he shouted to the men in the back of the truck. "Where's the ammo for this?"

"Gwen threw it away."

"What?"

"When she stole...I mean confiscated that weapon, she emptied the bullets out of that metal thing."

Sam threw open the bolt. A single bullet ejected from the chamber and fell at his feet. He would have one chance. He picked it up and ran back to the boulder where Hallie was standing.

"Can you still see him?"

"Yes...but that gator is going to kill him! It's biting his leg," she was getting frantic.

"I've got to try to shoot it from here."

Sam put the rifle butt to his shoulder, pressed his cheek to the stock and peered through the scope. He blinked to focus his vision. In the cross hairs he could see Mitch clearly. He was

189

wedged in the rocks near the water's edge. The gator had clamped onto the blood soaked elastic cuff of his riding pants. The fabric stretched each time the gator pulled. The beast moved slowly and deliberately, as if savoring a certain victory. Sam picked the center of the reptile's huge head as his target. He tried to steady the rifle. The image in the scope wouldn't hold still. Between the motion of the gator and his precarious stance, he knew he could easily blow Mitch's leg off if he missed.

"Shoot it!" Hallie pleaded.

"I can't get a good shot! Stand in front of me...I can steady the gun on your shoulder."

Hallie did as she was told.

"Put your fingers in your ears!"

Sam carefully trained the rifle on the gator. "Hold your breath," he whispered. The image settled down. Sam felt a knot in his stomach building. He took a deep breath and held it. As he slowly exhaled, his finger tightened on the trigger. The force of the recoil knocked him backwards off the boulder.

Down below, Mitch heard the shot. At the same instant, he was splattered with blood and bits of hide. Suddenly, the pulling on his leg stopped. It was replaced by a strange sound. It reminded him of a fish flopping on the bottom of a boat. Only much louder. With his last ounce of strength, Mitch looked back over his shoulder. The gator was spinning round and round. Its body arched and twisted, throwing blood and gore as it smashed against the rocky ground toward him. The last thing Mitch saw was the thick scaly tail coming down at his head. Then everything went black.

CHAPTER XXII

Mitch slowly became aware that he was no longer lying on rocks. His mouth tasted like chemicals. Each breath brought a wave of pain to his chest. A steady ache pushed in at his temples. Mitch had no idea where he was. The red glow coming through his closed eyelids was creating a dizzying light show in his skull. When he dozed off, he dreamed cartoon dreams. After a while, he noticed that someone was holding his left hand. His name drifted to him as if on a distant breeze. The voice came closer. It was familiar and comforting, yet confusing. He opened his parched lips to speak.

"Mom?" he whispered.

"It's me, Mitch," Hallie answered.

Mitch slowly digested the information.

"Where am I?"

"You're in the hospital...you got hurt pretty bad, but the docs fixed you up. You've been here three days."

He tried to look at her, but he couldn't open his eyes.

"Am I blind?"

"No, you're not blind...there's some gauze over your eyes so the light doesn't hurt so bad. You got a concussion from that alligator. He tore up your leg, too."

"Bet it was the gator I used to throw rocks at."

"You did what?...Hmmm, I guess paybacks are hell. Anyway, Sam says you're invited to a cookout when you're up and around. A certain alligator is on the menu."

"No kidding."

"If you're good, we'll make you a new pair of riding boots out of the hide."

Mitch raised his right hand. It felt large and clumsy.

"Your hand's all bandaged up. You had some pretty bad burns. Even your lungs got burned. That's why you couldn't breathe. They hope to get you out of intensive care in a few days."

The events of the race day continued to crystallize in Mitch's mind. He remembered the stranger he tried to save...and Rusty.

"Hallie, did Rusty try to do anything to you?"

"No...but I, well...I stabbed him."

Mitch was too drowsy to show his surprise. "You found out he killed Mark?"

"No, no...his cousin did it. He was that crazy man that drowned in the pit. Thad Henry was his name. Rusty was involved, but he didn't want Mark killed. The police are going to charge him with something, I suppose. I stabbed him by accident. He's in this hospital too, one floor up. I just came from there."

"Let me get this straight...the killer was the guy I tried to help at the quarry?"

"You tried to help him?"

"Yeah...but I couldn't keep him from falling."

"I'm sorry Mitch. It must have been awful."

"If I ever have another day like that, promise you'll put me out of my misery."

"I promise," she smiled.

"Thanks a lot."

The door behind Hallie slowly opened. Rusty McInster walked in. His abdomen was wrapped in bandages.

"He awake yet?"

"Yes...what are you doing up?"

"I got tired of layin' around."

"You're going to pull those stitches loose."

"Naw...it hardly even hurts. You look like hell, Mitch...all those tubes and wires and shit."

"You're both really cheering me up."

"I just wanted to tell you how sorry I was that I got mixed up in all this. I guess I didn't know

194

my cousin as well as I thought I did. None of this was supposed to happen."

"You better hope the police believe you." Mitch said.

Rusty looked down at the floor. Hallie put her hand on his shoulder. "It'll be alright."

She turned to Mitch. "I've got to go see Mel Coburn this afternoon. He ended up in the hospital too."

"What happened?" Mitch asked.

"It's a long story...he got beat up, sun stroke...I'll tell you all about it later. But he's a lot better now...I think he wants to go over my research before he heads for Tallahassee. I'll come back this evening to see you."

"You know where to find me."

Hallie leaned over and kissed his forehead. "See ya."

She turned to leave. "You should go back to bed, Rusty."

"In a little while. I want to talk to Mitch some more."

"Okay, but don't wear him out."

Rusty's eyes followed Hallie intently as she went out the door.

"That's one fine piece of girl flesh," he said.

Mitch didn't like the tone of his voice.

"Don't you ever give up?"

Rusty snorted harshly in reply. "Me...give

195

up...when it comes to things I want? No way."

Mitch heard Rusty move one of the chairs away from the bed. He heard it bump against the door.

"See Mitch, you did me a big favor. That cousin of mine...he just got too carried away. Fucker wanted Hallie for himself...after he promised he'd help me with my plan. But you fixed him good."

"Your plan?"

Rusty turned up the radio next to the bed, then leaned over Mitch, speaking through a wicked sneer.

"You don't think that stupid hick Thad planned this all out? It was my idea from the get go. Sure, he tried to double-cross me, and you screwed it up some, but it's still going to work."

"Turn that thing down...what the hell are you talking about?"

"Don't you get it? Hallie's going to be my girl. She feels real sorry about stabbing me. And I know just how to get rid of her guilt."

"You're out of your mind."

Rusty laughed. "No, Mitch...I'm not out of my mind. But you are if you think you're getting out of here alive. You're gonna' take a turn for the worse."

Mitch reached to pull the gauze off his eyes. Rusty grabbed his wrist and pinned it to the bed.

Mitch tried to yell for help, but he couldn't shout above the radio. Rusty leaped on top of him. He yanked the pillow free and stuffed it against Mitch's face. Sitting on his chest, Rusty pressed the pillow down with both hands. Mitch tried to push him off, but he didn't have the strength. Rusty put one elbow against Mitch's throat. Mitch felt his windpipe compress. His lungs burned as he tried to take a breath. His head began to feel like it was swarming with bees. As the darkness started to creep over him, he quit struggling.

The duty nurse had just returned to her post from attending other patients. She was annoyed that so many of them had buzzed her but had no recollection of doing so. As she sat down with a crossword puzzle, an alarm beeper went off. She glanced at the control panel. One of her patients had quit breathing. She hurled her heavy frame around the desk and ran down the corridor. As she passed another nurse she shouted; "Pulmonary arrest, room 227, get a crash cart... stat!"

She tried to open the door, but it was stuck. She threw her weight against it. It burst open, sending the chair spinning across the room. She stood in shock, staring at the other patient on top of Mitch. It took her a moment to realize what was happening.

"Get off him!" she yelled, lunging forward. She got her arms around Rusty's shoulders and threw him off the bed. "Orderly!"

Rusty scrambled to his feet and ran. The nurse turned to Mitch and quickly found his pulse. She flipped open a pocket mirror and placed it in front of his mouth and nose. It didn't fog up. She grabbed Mitch's head, tilted it back and closed her mouth over his. It didn't take her long to breathe the color back into him. By the time the other nurse arrived with the equipment, Mitch was breathing on his own.

"Call security!" the duty nurse instructed. "Another patient was in here trying to kill Mr. Clanton."

By a process of elimination, the hospital staff figured out who the attacker was. But by that time, Rusty was nowhere to be found. A search of his room revealed that he had changed back into street clothes before he fled. The police took down what information they could, then put out an all points bulletin for Russell R. McInster.

Charlie Dorge arrived at the hospital a short time later. He was directed to intensive care. Mitch was dozing off as Dorge entered his room. The painkillers they had given him had taken the edge off his latest brush with death.

The detective shook him. "Hey Clanton, come to for a minute, will ya?"

Mitch slowly rolled his head to face him.

"Looks like I was right all along about that

little dirtbag. The Alabama police finally saw fit to send us the information we requested. He's got a respectable rap sheet. Arrested six times, spent one summer in a mental institution. Only one decent conviction, for aggravated assault. And guess what? It was over a girl. I knew I had him pegged!"

Dorge snapped his fingers in front of Mitch's face. "You with me, Clanton?"

"Ummmhuh..." Mitch mumbled. "What about your skunk ape theory...?"

"Sure, sure...now look, Rusty was your client...do you know where I can find him?"

"His trailer?"

"No luck there. He grabbed some of his stuff and took off. I thought you might know where he would go to hide out. He seems to be related to half the population of the river swamp. But they don't exactly cooperate with the police out there. You know anything that might help?"

"What about Alabama?"

"Yeah, there's a good chance he might try to leave the state. But wherever he went, he's going to be conspicuous with that hole in his gut. Your girlfriend got him good with that pigsticker of hers." The deputy swung an imaginary knife forward, making a guttural sound.

"Charlie...could you put a deputy on her...I don't think she's safe with him loose out there."

"I'm way ahead of you. I've got one of my

best stakeout guys watching her. I just hope he's dumb enough to try for her."

"You never quit, do you Charlie?"

"Quit what?"

CHAPTER XXIII

Over the next six days, Mitch slowly regained his strength. On the morning he was to be released from the hospital, the head nurse brought him a newspaper.

"I thought you might be interested in this story," she said, folding the paper in quarters and handing it to him.

Mitch had to hold the paper at nearly arms length to read it.

"You should get some reading glasses." she said as she turned to leave.

Mitch scowled at her backside, then squinted at the paper. Under a photo of the smoldering ruins of a house was the headline: "Local Suspect Believed Dead In Alabama Shootout". It continued:

"Alabama police reported on Monday that a fugitive from Florida is believed dead in a bloody shootout with federal agents. The violence began when a Caucasian man matching the description of Russell McInster held up the Security Bank in Maple Hills, Alabama. A high speed chase ended when the suspect took refuge in a remote farmhouse in rural Primrose County. Federal agents were called in when the sheriff's department learned that the farmhouse was occupied by at least two dozen heavily armed members of a white separatist militia.

When agents of the Alcohol, Tobacco and Firearms Bureau arrived at the scene, they were met by a volley of automatic gunfire from the house. The federal agents returned fire. One of the shots is believed to have struck a propane tank in the kitchen area, causing a massive explosion and fireball. None of the suspects were able to escape the gunfire and the resulting blaze. Two federal agents were wounded, one seriously.

Alabama authorities are examining the remains of the suspects to determine their identities. The forensic investigation is expected to take several days. Dental records of Mr. McInster are being sought at this time. Russell McInster was wanted by local police for attempted murder, aggravated assault and his possible connection to the murder of a Florida man named Mark Jemison..."

Mitch began to read further when he heard someone enter the room. Hallie had come to drive him home.

"Did you see this article?" he asked.

"Yes."

"Looks like he found his Armageddon."

"I still find it hard to believe," Hallie said, shaking her head.

"I guess it's hard to tell what makes some people tick. Anyway, I'm glad we don't have to worry about him anymore."

"I suppose...but the whole mess is so sad."

Hallie took the newspaper from him and tossed it on the chair.

"Enough of that," she said. "You ready for some assisted living?"

"What do you mean?"

"You don't remember?"

"Remember what?"

"You said I should move into your house."

"Oh, yeah...but I was lying about the motorhome."

"I might let you stay in the house too...if you're good."

"I'll be good...I promise."

"You better."

Hallie leaned over him, tilted his chin back and kissed him hard. Her perfume made his head swim.

"I may need a lot of therapy," he grinned.

Hallie slid her hand inside his hospital gown.

"I've got just what the doctor ordered," she whispered. "Now get your crutch, get dressed and let's get you out of this place."

As they were getting his belongings together, Sam and Paul walked in.

"We heard you were bustin' out today."

"You got that right."

"Need a lift home?"

"Sorry...just got a better offer."

Sam feigned hurt feelings. "And after I saved your life."

"It's not that I don't appreciate it, Sam... but you're just not as good a kisser."

"You never gave me a chance."

"I'm telling your wife on you. By the way, what ever happened to those jerks that messed up the race?"

"The guys got off pretty easy. The judge ordered them to do a couple hundred hours of community service. They're going to work on some sea turtle protection project. The ringleader of the group is due in court next week. We heard she was found wandering down the highway half naked and covered with poison ivy. Kept ranting about some wild man that held her captive."

Mitch just smiled.

The nurse arrived with a wheelchair. "Time to go, Mr. Clanton."

The town seemed somehow different to Mitch on the way home. Outwardly, it looked the same, but he found himself paying closer attention to what people were doing. Everyone seemed occupied in their own little world. He wondered how many of them appreciated just being alive. He made a mental note to not take anything for granted anymore.

"How's your study going?"

"Good...Mr. Coburn decided to let me do it my way."

"Great."

"You guys aren't getting off scott free, though. I'll have some suggestions on future course layouts."

"Fair enough. How's Mel doing?"

"He fine now. And they found his horse. But I think he's permanently disillusioned with Florida."

"Why's that?"

"Well, first there was the run in with Thad Henry and that crazy anti-hunting group. And the heat stroke didn't do much for his outlook. Then he found out that a big land purchase he helped put together went sour."

"How so?"

"A big citrus company stepped in at the last minute and outbid the state. They're clearing the land to grow a new type of cold-hardy oranges."

"Too bad."

"Yeah, Mr. Coburn said he would turn in his resignation pretty soon. He's going to head out to Montana...said he needs to find a place where he can ride his horse to his heart's content...and not get sun stroked."

"Wonder if he's heard about frostbite?"

Halfway across town, Hallie turned off the main road.

"I need to stop by my apartment and get White Fang."

She pulled up to her place and hopped out. Mitch watched her trot up to her apartment. He liked the feeling of Hallie coming to live with him. He hoped it would last.

CHAPTER XXIV

Hallie loaded White Fang into the cage in the back of her truck. As she got behind the wheel, Mitch noticed a scrap of paper in her hand.

"What's that?"

"I had a message on my answering machine...it was some old lady."

"Somebody you know?"

"No. But she said she knew who I was."

"What did she say?"

"She said she found some photos of me... wondered if I wanted them back."

"Where is she?"

"Out near Possum Bluff. She gave directions but didn't leave a phone number."

"You going to get them?"

"Of course...you want to come with?"

"Sure, it's a nice day for a drive in the country. I've been cooped up too long anyway."

"Maybe we can stop by the spring on the way back."

"Mrs. Robinson, you're trying to seduce

me."

"I just wanted to practice the mermaid thing...you know, like before. You never know, I could land a job at Silver Springs."

"Yeah...you could learn to eat a banana underwater," he grinned.

Hallie socked him.

"Mitchell!"

"Ow!"

The road to Possum Bluff had never been paved. The crushed limerock had turned to dust under decades of old pickup trucks, rusty sedans and hoofbeats. The county occasionally graded the road, but the washboard always returned, as if by some natural process of the earth's crust. The residents paid it no mind.

Mitch wasn't enjoying the jolting ride. Every bounce of Hallie's truck brought painful memories of his recent injuries. Hallie slowed for the bigger bumps, but she couldn't miss them all. "Are you sure she was on the level?"

"She sounded like a nice old lady. A little strange, but I'm sure she was telling the truth."

"I wonder how she got your name."

"From the newspaper stories, I guess. Anyway, she said I would want these photos."

"Are they all of you?"

"Apparently. She found them in a box along

this road."

"I wonder if we should have called the sheriff's department."

"Not till I get a look at the photos, thank you very much."

"Okay, but let's treat them like evidence. We don't need Dorge charging us with tampering."

"You worry too much."

"Occupational hazard."

They turned onto a narrower dirt road. The pot holes and washouts were deeper. The truck tires spun as mud sloshed against the wheel wells.

"You sure we're on the right track?"

"I think so. We should be pretty close."

"To the edge of the earth?"

Just then they rounded a curve into an oak hammock. Spanish moss hung down everywhere, almost hiding the tin-roofed shacks on either side of the road. In the distance, the St. Johns River flowed gracefully north. The place looked deserted.

"She said to go to the main house. I guess it's that one." Hallie pointed to a slightly bigger structure with a wide porch. She parked the truck in the shade of the oaks.

Mitch reached for his single metal crutch behind the seat. As they got out, a lazy coon hound came out from under the house. It stood and stretched, then walked toward them, tail wagging. White Fang gave a low growl of disapproval.

"You be good," Hallie said. "This is his yard."

She bent down toward the dog to give it a pat. A voice from the house startled her upright.

"He won't bother you none."

It was the voice from the telephone. The old lady stayed behind the screen door, in the dim light of the house.

"Hello, there." Mitch said.

"You the young lady from the pictures?" she asked Hallie.

"Yes Ma'am, I guess so."

"Who's this with you?"

"A friend of mine, Mitchell Clanton."

"Mitch Clanton...I read about him in the papers, too. Didn't know you was bringing company."

"I'm sorry."

"He your sweetheart?"

Hallie smiled. "You could say that."

"In that case, you can come in."

They pushed past the dog and went up the sagging steps. Mitch saw that the house was not made of brick as it appeared. Instead, there was old vinyl flooring with a brick pattern nailed up over the ancient cypress siding. The screen door creaked as it slowly opened in front of them. As their eyes adjusted, they surveyed the main room. There was very little furniture. One small couch, one old wooden rocker and a weathered table. A single light fixture hung by a wire in the center of the room. At one end, embers in a fireplace smoldered under a black iron kettle. What the room lacked in furniture it made up for in clutter. The walls were lined with shelves of all sizes. They were jammed with an incredible array of jars, bags, tins, bottles and objects too strange to identify. It smelled like a natural history museum.

They turned toward the old woman. Half-hidden beneath straggled gray hair, her dark sunken eyes punctuated the pale, leathery skin. The folds of her neck made her look like a human mushroom. She spoke first.

"I'm fixin' some tea, please have some with me."

"That would be nice, thank you," said Hallie.

"How about you, young man?"

"No, thank you."

"Oh please, I don't get visitors very often."

"Well, okay...I guess I could have a cup."

"Good...I'll be right back."

The old lady smiled and started toward the adjoining kitchen.

"Do you need any help?" Hallie asked.

"No thank you, dear...I can manage. You two make yourselves comfortable."

They took a seat on the sofa. After quite a

few minutes, she returned with an ancient china tea set.

"Here you are, dear," she said, handing a cup to Hallie. "And one for you, young man."

Mitch took the cup. He struggled to smile as he looked at the stained cup and its filmy, brown contents.

"What kind is it?" he asked lamely, buying time.

"It's a special herb tea. I hope you like it. Sorry I don't have any sugar."

Mitch and Hallie stared at each other as the old woman proceeded to drink. Hallie raised her cup and took a swallow. Mitch hoped he would gain some insight from her reaction to the vile looking brew. But she remained expressionless.

"Interesting flavor," Hallie said.

Mitch shrugged his shoulders and took a sip. It was all he could do to keep it down. He doubted that a whole cane field of sugar would make the stuff palatable. He smiled weakly and nodded in false approval. The old lady smiled back at him and began rocking slowly in her chair.

Mitch was desperate to avoid drinking any more. He glanced down and noticed a crack in the floorboards of the house. The old coon hound was directly below him.

"What are all those containers for?" Mitch asked, gesturing toward the shelves on the far wall.

As the old lady turned to look, Mitch poured some tea through the crack. The dog moved.

"Those are my herbal medicines. I use them to make poltices and other remedies for the local people."

"You're a doctor?"

"Some folks say I am. And some call me a witch doctor, too. What I do was passed down through generations. There's more power in plants and potions than most people ever imagine."

"Interesting."

"But I'm a dying breed. Nobody wants to take the time to learn the old ways. Too easy to use store bought. I don't know who'll take care of folks 'round here when I'm gone."

Mitch faked another swallow.

"It was very kind of you to call me," Hallie said.

"Nothin' of the kind. I just wanted to set things right."

"Can I see the photographs?"

"Of course, I'll go fetch 'em."

As the old lady made her way out of the room, Mitch and Hallie exchanged wide-eyed looks. Mitch poured the rest of the tea down the crack. A thick sediment stayed in the cup.

"Can you believe her?" Hallie whispered.

"I will if you will."

"How about this tea?"

"She must not have any tastebuds."

They fell silent when they heard her coming back. She sat down in the rocker with a green military ammunitions box in her lap. Undoing the latch, she pulled out a handful of photographs.

"These are the pictures of you."

She handed them to Hallie, who began to thumb through them. She held them so Mitch couldn't see. All of them were taken during Hallie's field work. Some of them were personal. Hallie separated those photos from the rest.

"Is this all of them?"

"There's just one more you need to see."

The old lady slowly pulled out the last photograph. She laid it in Hallie's hand. It was obviously much older than the rest. The edges were bent and discolored, and the image was not as clear. There were two people in the photo. Hallie immediately recognized one of them as the old lady. Only twenty years younger. She squinted at the other figure. It was a boy who looked very familiar. Then she knew who it was. Hallie could feel the hair on the back of her neck begin to rise. Without looking up, Hallie said, "This is Rusty McInster, isn't it?"

Instead of a verbal answer, Hallie heard two clicks. As she looked up, she was looking down the double barrels of an old pearl-handled derringer.

"Miiiitch," Hallie breathed.

Mitch had seen the old lady pull the weapon from the ammo box. But he had been unable to move to stop her. He tried to warn Hallie, but he couldn't make his jaw work. Gravity seemed to have multiplied tenfold. It drove him into the sofa and held him down. His stomach felt like it would erupt. He thought he could hear his heart slowing down.

"What's wrong, Mitch?"

He couldn't answer. Suddenly, Hallie felt weak and dizzy. She put her head down between her knees.

"What's happening?"

The old lady's voice took on a hard edge. "I'm just finishing what you started, dearie. Hope you enjoyed your tea."

She reached over with surprising strength and grabbed Hallie by the hair.

"We're going for a little walk."

CHAPTER XXV

The bright sun hurt Hallie's eyes as she was forced down the steps of the old house. The woman led her around back, where the ground went uphill toward a small clearing. Hallie struggled to keep her balance. Her senses had gone haywire. Objects danced and swirled in her vision. Sounds were magnified. The wind through the oak leaves sounded like a hundred waterfalls. Even the hot sun felt strangely cool. If Hallie had ever experimented with psilocybin and peyote, she might have recognized the effects. The beauty of the day belied the terror that she was experiencing.

"What did you do to Mitch?"

"Castor bean extract and opiate. It's a slow but sure death. Justice must be served."

"Why...why are you doing this?" Hallie cried.

"You'll see...keep moving."

The old woman pushed her onward, to the top of the hill. Hallie swayed as she tried to focus on her surroundings. A shove from behind sent her to her knees. Her outstretched hands came down on something hard. Leaning forward, she could see it was a small headstone. She was in the middle of a family cemetery.

The woman took her by the hair again and led her like a dog toward another grave. This one was fresh.

"Read it!" she ordered.

Hallie put her face close. She used her fingers to help make out the roughcut lettering.

"RUSSELL R. MCINSTER...BORN 12-20-66, DIED 3-24-98."

"That's my grandson down there."

"Why did you bring me here?"

"I raised him after his momma died giving him life. I put everything into makin' sure he got a chance in life. First child in our family ever went to high school."

The old woman's voice started to break.

"But he never forgot his roots...always came back to me when he needed help. And I never let him down...till this last time. He was so bad with fever I couldn't make it right. And now he's gone...all on account of you."

"But I never meant to..."

"Don't lie to me! He told me all about you. How you led him on. How you cheated on him with that man back there...the one who killed my nephew. And how you finally put a knife in him."

"But it wasn't like that."

"You sayin' it wasn't your knife what killed him."

"But it was an accident...I didn't mean..."

"Enough! Tell him you're sorry."

"What?"

"You heard me...tell him you're sorry you did him wrong."

"But..."

"You tell him, gal, and I might let you live."

"You've got this all wrong..."

"I know what I know! You crawl over here...now!"

As Hallie tried to look up, she nearly passed out. She crawled toward the woman. Suddenly the ground was gone. She felt along the edge of a deep hole next to Rusty's grave.

"That one's for you. Rusty couldn't have you in life...I aim to see you're with him for eternity."

"Please, you can't do this..."

"You should have thought of that before you killed him. An eye for an eye..."

The old woman put the derringer against the back of Hallie's head. Hallie shut her eyes. The woman pulled the trigger.

Click.

The cartridge didn't fire. She put her finger on the second trigger and squeezed. A flash of metal came down on her arm as the gun went off. The bullet buried itself in the ground next to Hallie's face. The force of swinging the crutch carried Mitch into the old woman. She looked up in surprise as she went headlong into the open grave. Mitch fell heavily to the ground.

Hallie opened her eyes. The gunshot left powder burns on her cheek. Her ears were filled with noise. Mitch reached toward her and cradled her head in his arms.

"Did she hurt you?"

"No," she said, sniffing back tears. "But she said she poisoned you. We've got to get help."

"I only had a sip. It didn't stay down long. I think I'll be okay."

Hallie rolled sideways, looking into the open grave.

"She's not moving."

Mitch pulled himself around to look. His stomach suddenly convulsed, sending the last of the witch's brew down on the old woman. The back of her head was resting on a shoulder blade.

"Neck's broken," he said without emotion.

CHAPTER XXVI

The alarm clock buzzed annoyingly on Mitch's bedside table. He rolled over and whacked the button on top. This was the day they were going fishing. It was still pitch dark outside. He stretched across the bed to wake Hallie. She wasn't there. Then he noticed the shower was running. Lying on his back, staring into the darkness, he felt terrific. His recovery was almost complete. The doctors had been wrong about him needing a kidney transplant. He had fought off the poison with no lasting effects.

Everything else was going well too. The investigation into the deaths of Thad Henry, Rusty McInster and the old lady, Elizabeth Cray, had concluded that no wrongdoing had occurred. He had even managed to get Jerry and himself exonerated for their actions on the day of The Alligator. The blackjack Dorge had used on Hallie had turned the tide in their favor. The judge said the detective was lucky he wasn't facing charges himself. The county sheriff put Dorge on temporary beach patrol to rethink his role as a public servant.

Hallie came out of the bathroom and turned on the light. "Okay, Rip Van Winkle, time to get up."

Mitch covered his eyes, rolled over and pretended to go back to sleep.

"You heard me, Mitchell. Rise and shine!"

She leaned over to pull the covers off. Mitch quickly grabbed her around her naked waist and wrestled her into bed.

"Okay, lover boy...you promised to take me fishing."

"Just trying to wake up."

Hallie rolled on top of him. "I think part of you is already awake..."

By the time they drove down the ramp to the beach, a light offshore breeze was rippling the Atlantic. The sun was just beginning to emerge from the horizon. Orange clouds streaked toward the mainland, changing hue with the rising of the sun. Mitch pulled up to the posts marking the edge of the turtle nesting area and parked his new van. Except for a lone pickup truck and its three occupants in the distance, they were alone.

"What a morning," he said, taking a deep breath. "At last I get some real vacation time."

"This is nice," she agreed.

"Let's go over by the jetty. I know a place

where the flounder hang out this time of year."

"I catch 'em, you clean 'em," Hallie said, patting Mitch on the cheek.

They gathered their gear and headed toward the water's edge. After walking along the shore for a few hundred yards, Mitch stopped.

"This is the spot...I can smell them out there," he said, taking a deep breath.

"You can smell them?"

"Of course. They're fish, aren't they?"

"You're full of it!"

"We're both going to be full of it at dinner tonight."

"Then you better catch us some bait."

Mitch slipped the loop on the rope to his cast net around his left wrist. He coiled the rest of the rope in the same hand, then lifted the net by the plastic ring at the top. Grabbing the net in the middle, he clenched one of the lead weights in his teeth and tossed layers of mesh over his right forearm. Then he stalked the shoreline, looking for shiners. A small school was coming toward him. When they were in range, he spun around, flinging the net expertly over the baitfish. He pulled on the rope, which tightened the brails and closed the bottom of the net. Then he dragged it onto the shore, flopping with small silver bodies.

As he walked back toward Hallie, Mitch noticed a beach security vehicle coming down the ramp. It was a topless job with a yellow light attached to the rollbar. The driver turned toward them and stopped a short distance away. Charlie Dorge stepped out.

"Good Morning, Mitch...Miss Shugart."

Mitch stepped in front of Hallie.

"We don't want any trouble, Charlie."

"I'm not here to give you any trouble. In fact, I want to thank you."

"Thank us?"

"Yep. This assignment has been a godsend for me. The fresh sea air, peace and quiet, even quit smoking...I feel like a new man."

He extended his hand to Mitch. Mitch stared into the detective's eyes. He saw no signs of deceit, so he took the offered hand.

"You're serious," Mitch said in astonishment.

"That's right," Dorge said. "No hard feelings. Even my blood pressure is down. My doctor says I'll live ten years longer if I stay with this job. Nothing is going to stress me out any more."

"We're happy for you," said Hallie.

"Well, don't let me keep you from your fishing. That bait needs to stay in the water."

Mitch emptied the net into a bait pen he had made from a clothes basket.

"By the way, have either of you seen

anyone out here this morning. I got a call that some folks were sneaking around on the beach last night."

"There were three people over there a little while ago," Mitch said, pointing down the beach. At first all he saw was the truck. Then he saw three forms just barely visible, down on their hands and knees. They appeared to be digging.

"There they are."

"Thanks, I'll check them out. You two have a great day."

"Same to you."

The detective drove in the direction of the three crouched figures. As he got closer, he saw the mass of bumper stickers. It was the same green truck that he had chased at the Alligator Enduro. The three people were carefully placing something in a hole they had dug. Dorge stepped on the gas and hurried toward the pickup. Off to the left, he saw the remains of a large animal. It was a sea turtle. One flipper seemed to be stuck to a metal object buried in the sand. Raccoons had torn the flesh from anything that stuck out from the shell. As he sped along, he noticed a crumpled plastic decal on the sand. He craned his neck to read it as he went by. He mouthed the words: "Warning, severe tire dam......"

He was cut short by the sound of four tires blowing out in quick succession. His vehicle careened from side to side as he fought to regain control. He was now driving on the rims. The two men and the woman dropped what they were doing and bolted toward their pickup. Just as they jumped in, Charlie Dorge rammed the front of their truck. His radiator burst, raining hot coolant on the detective.

"Freeze, you bastards!" he screamed at them. The three sat motionless in the truck. Dorge reached instinctively for his gun, then realized he didn't have one. He pulled out his nightstick and approached the vehicle. In the back of the truck were half a dozen tire shredding devices.

"What the hell are you people doing," he demanded.

"Someone's got to stop the driving on the beach...to save the turtles," the woman replied.

"Tell that to the turtle you killed back there."

"The shredders were too shallow...we were fixing that problem."

"The only thing you're going to fix is..."

Before he could finish his sentence, the man nearest him threw open the truck door, knocking the detective to the sand. They leaped out and sprinted toward the water. Dorge got up and ran after them. They turned and went south, toward the jetty. As they ran past Mitch and Hallie, Charlie Dorge was cursing at the top of his lungs.

Hallie turned to watch them go by. Mitch didn't seem to notice.

"What on earth do you suppose..."

"Didn't see a thing," he said, putting on a fresh bait. Mitch made a long cast, just short of a small sandbar. After a few moments of staring out to sea, he turned to Hallie.

"You know what I like about the beach?"

"What's that?"

"No spiders."

If You Have Enjoyed this Book and Would Like Additional Copies, Please Ask for This Book at Your Local Bookstore or Order Directly From:

stubradow@aol.com

Red Quill Publishing
~~P.O. Box 4191~~
Enterprise, FL 32725-0191

Send check or money order for $6.95 per book, plus $2.00 per order for postage and handling. No cash or C.O.D.'s please. Allow four to six weeks for delivery. Be sure to include your complete mailing address with your order.